THE LYING GAME

A totally addictive romantic suspense that you won't be able to put down

Faith Martin writing as
MAXINE BARRY

D0962414

JOFFE
BOOKS

First published by Joffe Books, London 2020
www.joffebooks.com

First published in Great Britain 2006

© Maxine Barry 2006, 2020

**Please join our mailing list for free Kindle books and
new releases.**

www.joffebooks.com

ISBN 978-1-78931-388-8

ONE

Oriana Foster bent down to zip up her bag. In it she had a pair of very worn and faded jeans, two plain white blouses, a dark-green knitted cardigan, given to her by an aunt long since dead, some underthings, and a toiletries bag. In the toiletries bag was a toothbrush and a half-empty tube of toothpaste. Other than what she stood up in, it was all she had.

Maybe.

She zipped up the cheap holdall, something she'd bought with her wages from her job in the kitchens, and looked around. Whitewashed walls. Posters of green fields and rivers on the wall. A bunk bed, attached to the wall by rusty brackets.

She turned and walked to the door. Outside, on the landing, she heard the usual volume of noise coming from below. In the rec room, two women were playing table tennis, and playing very well at that. One, Vera McKloskey, was an expert. She'd been playing the game for years. Twenty-two years, some said, although others derided that as a mere rumour.

Oriana walked slowly down the iron staircase, her feet, clad in a pair of battered trainers, still somehow managing to make a resounding racket as she negotiated the metal stairs.

Everywhere around her there was noise. Her own footsteps. Voices. Clangs, and assorted clatters. It never seemed to stop. Even at night calls came out of the walls: women's voices wishing others goodnight, passing on gossip, or even, sometimes, threats.

Oriana glanced up as a middle-aged woman approached her. Known to one and all as Miss Clunes, she was dressed in a smart navy-blue skirt and white blouse. She smiled. 'Well, Orrie, looks like this is it, then. Got everything?'

Oriana glanced down ruefully at her small bag. 'I think so, miss,' she said quietly. Then smiled. 'Any Rembrandts I may have forgotten, or diamond tiaras I might have left behind, will just have to be forwarded.'

A girl, who looked barely sixteen, suddenly giggled. She was sitting by a radiator, reading *Hello!* magazine. 'That's a good one that is. Tiara. Hey, Shaz, we'll have to remember that.' She spoke to another teenage girl, busily smoking a cigarette with far too much concentration. Oriana looked at her and wondered what she was on. And where she'd got it. Then she shrugged. It was none of her business any more. Any of it.

Miss Clunes also looked thoughtfully at Shaz, who was very much her business.

'Said all your goodbyes then?' the older woman glanced at Oriana quickly. 'Sorry you can't see Sandra. But she'll soon get back on enhanced, and then you can write.'

Oriana nodded. But she doubted if her friend would want her to write. She'd asked her not to. Oriana understood. She understood perfectly.

Miss Clunes walked across the dark green linoleum floor to a heavy steel door and unlocked it with one of the keys from the set chained to her waist. Behind her, Oriana could feel the eyes watching her. Most were friendly. All were envious.

As Miss Clunes opened the door and Oriana walked through it, a chorus of calls sounded out behind her. 'Good luck, Orrie.' 'Lucky cow!' 'Don't do anything I wouldn't.' And others, some ribald, some wistful. Oriana turned and smiled back at them, but then quickly looked forward as Miss Clunes relocked the door and walked briskly ahead.

The passageway seemed long and ill-lit, but Oriana didn't mind. Today, she wasn't going to mind anything.

Yet another locked door greeted the arrival of the corridor's end, and Oriana shifted her bag into her other hand as she waited. It was amazing, she thought, vaguely surprised, just how patient she felt. How long had she been marking this day off in her mental calendar? How many dreams of this moment had plagued her over the years? Hadn't this moment taken on the significance of her birthday, Christmas and Doomsday all rolled into one? And now that it was here, she felt . . . well . . . patient. Waiting for the door to be unlocked. Walking behind Miss Clunes, one of her favourites, to a small, non-descript office. Waiting whilst a civilian secretary retrieved her file.

Oriana sighed and glanced out of the window, but of course, all she could see was the courtyard, a part of the gardens, and a high wall.

She could wait. She was good at waiting.

'Will you check the contents please, Orrie, and then sign here?' Miss Clunes asked, and Oriana, with a start, saw that she was holding out a large brown envelope towards her.

It had been years since she'd last seen it.

Oriana took it to the desk and emptied it out. Her purse looked back at her. Inside it were a few notes and some change. She knew, if she cared to check the inventory, that it would tell her exactly how much it amounted to, but she didn't bother. Next to it, her now outdated passport. Oriana didn't open it — didn't want to see the girl she'd been before this nightmare began. Instead she picked up a small gold watch. It had stopped at 3.32, and she wondered if it could possibly still work. Her mother had bought it for her for her birthday, her first 'grown-up' present. It was Swiss, and was still, in those days, a real watch, with no battery needed. Absently, without much hope, Oriana wound it up and put it on her wrist.

Miss Clunes watched her, wondering what could possibly be going through her mind. She'd seen many girls go through this, of course. It was part of her working day. Most of them were excited. Some defiant. A few even frightened. But if somebody had offered to pay her a thousand pounds, Miss Clunes couldn't have told them what Oriana Foster was thinking.

She was a strange girl, in many ways, Miss Clunes mused. Quiet. But not weak. You had to watch out for the weak ones. They could get into serious trouble. She watched as the slender wrist was held up to a small, rather delicate-looking ear.

'Is it working?' she asked, curious.

Oriana smiled, shaking her head in disbelief. 'You might not think so, but it actually is,' she said happily. She pushed her hand into the envelope once more, and her face, all at once, seemed to close down.

Miss Clunes tensed automatically. She was a very observant woman, and easily picked up any signs of danger brewing. But all that Oriana Foster now held in her hand was a small gold heart-shaped pendant, and she slowly relaxed.

'Sentimental value, Orrie?' she asked gently.

Oriana's fingers closed around the locket and she slipped it into one of the side pockets of the holdall. 'It doesn't matter,' Oriana said flatly. It had been given to her a long time ago. By a man.

She checked that the envelope was now empty, and folding it neatly in half, handed it back to the older woman. 'Thank you, miss,' she said simply.

Miss Clunes nodded and walked with her to the door. It was locked, of course, and Oriana waited, with yet more patience, as this was dealt with. Then they were outside, in an inner courtyard. Some cars, belonging to staff with a much-prized parking permit, lined walls blackened with centuries of city grime. The building was old. Some reformers thought much too old. Outside, in the courtyard, a man waited. He, too, was dressed in navy blue.

'Well, goodbye then, Orrie,' Miss Clunes said, looking at her sharply. 'Be good now. You have the addresses we gave you, and know what you have to do?'

Oriana nodded and patted the other pocket of her hold-all, where several papers were stored. 'Safe and sound,' she promised softly.

'I don't want to see you in here again, now,' Miss Clunes added grimly, as the man outside unlocked the iron gate.

Halfway through it, Oriana Foster looked back at Miss Clunes. She had a kind face, but it was older than it should have been. The eyes were wise, but hard. Oriana didn't flinch from them. 'It's all right, miss,' she said softly. 'I won't be back.'

And Miss Clunes believed her.

How often had she heard those words? From how many faces, young and old, brave and defeated? But from this really quite beautiful young woman, Miss Clunes found herself believing them. She nodded once, then turned and walked away.

'This way.' The male voice was firm, a little truculent. Oriana obeyed at once, and followed him across the paved yard to the final door, a huge set of iron-studded double gates set in an equally huge brick wall.

Oriana felt her blood begin to tingle. It heated, just a little, and seemed to move more quickly around her veins. Time stretched and sped up simultaneously. Her breath was uncomfortably trapped somewhere. She saw the key turn, heard it click. Saw the mass of wood begin to move. Through the crack came movement and colour. Cars. The door opened further and revealed a dusty cityscape, London on a hot May day. Her breath escaped.

'Off you go then.' Oriana nodded. 'Thank you,' she said quietly, and stepped outside.

And behind her, the doors of Falconbridge Women's Prison closed with a hard, dull finality.

For a minute, Oriana simply stood and looked around her. She had no coat, for the one she'd been wearing when she first came to this place had grown too small for her. She was only sixteen then. Since then, she'd filled out. Luckily the sun was shining, but for some reason she couldn't quite fathom, she felt cold.

A woman laden with Tesco shopping bags looked at her curiously, her gaze rising to the sign on the door behind her, then slewing anxiously away.

Oriana saw her walk a little faster and felt like weeping. She did no such thing of course. She couldn't remember the last time she'd cried. During the trial, probably. Instead, she turned on her heel and walked away, crossing the road, wondering where she was. She didn't know London at all. She'd been born and raised in a small country village, the only daughter of a railway worker and a school secretary.

She took the first bus which stopped and eventually found herself in Oxford Circus. From there, she reasoned, she should be able to find her way about, and using up some of the coins in her purse, which were themselves more than thirteen years old, bought herself a folding map from a newsagents, and found a cafe. Inside she ordered a Coke and took a seat.

It was strange how familiar yet otherworldly everything seemed. Nothing much seemed to have changed at all. Perhaps it was because people looked the same, no matter where you lived. A high-rise flat in Peckham. A semi-detached in Surbiton. A prison cell. People would always be people. But she expected there were some things she'd have to adjust to. For a start, the price of her Coke had nearly made her faint. And the expanse of glass which was the cafe window gave off a giddying sense of space.

For the first time in over thirteen years she could choose what to do. What to drink. Where to go.

There were no more locked doors.

Oriana sipped her Coke and looked outside for a long, long time.

In prison, it was noise which had seemed constant. Here, although there was certainly noise, it was movement which seemed constant. Cars, lorries, vans, bikes. All moving. People, hurrying here, hurrying there. Pigeons begging crumbs from people leaving the cafe with their takeaway food. Everything seemed to be moving, whilst Oriana felt strangely static. But she knew this feeling would wear off. She'd get used to it. People, she understood from first-hand experience, could get used to anything.

Given time.

The waitress wiped the table next to hers, glancing across at Oriana as she did so. Her cloth dashed across the bright yellow Formica with an ease born of practice. She was old, and her feet hurt, but something about the woman sitting so quietly, so still and wide-eyed, caught her attention. Usually customers didn't do that. They were just mouths to be fed, money machines to be milked and then passed on to the next milking station. But this woman was different, and the waitress couldn't figure out why. She was beautiful, of course, but she got all sorts in the cafe. Perhaps it was the short, curly blonde hair, the colour of cornsilk. You didn't see short curly hair much nowadays.

But it wasn't that. The girl was thin, too thin, in the waitress's opinion, her own proportions being more inclined to the well-padded, but she didn't think it was that either. Nowadays all the models looked like stick insects. Ah, she wasn't wearing any make-up. That was it. She looked so pale.

'Excuse me, luv, you just come out of hospital?' she heard herself asking bluntly.

Oriana turned startled eyes towards her. They were pale blue, and fringed by naturally dark lashes.

'No,' Oriana said simply. Just that.

In prison, it had been one of the first lessons she'd learned. Don't blab. Don't invade anyone's space. Don't ask questions. Don't say more than you need to. Watch your back. Always and ever, watch your back.

'Oh,' the waitress said, finding herself wrongfooted. She turned away quickly, muttering something about it being none of her business. She felt, for some odd reason, hurt.

Oriana would have been surprised to know this. And would have felt sorry. But, as it was, she simply turned to look at the map, spreading it out over the table and getting her bearings. She needed to find Naughton Street. There was a man there she needed to see. And urgently. Because she needed to know if it was true. If that letter, smuggled in to her by an ex-forger one cold February day nearly seven years ago, could possibly be true.

Because if it was . . .

She took the bus, of course, not daring to spend any more of her resources on a taxi fare. Odd to think that money might be the last, the very last thing, she need worry about.

Naughton Street, Oriana soon realized the moment she turned off a main street and stepped on to its quiet, leafy pavement, was above all a *respectable* street. Brass plaques gave the names of solicitors, doctors, chartered surveyors, accountants. There were even private homes and residences scattered amongst them. Black wrought-iron railings fenced off basement steps or smart gardens filled with small cherry trees or flowering shrubs.

A black cat, sat in a sunny patch on a low wall, miaowed at her in passing. It stopped Oriana dead in her tracks. It had been many years since she'd seen such a thing.

The cat stood up and stretched luxuriously, arching its back and yawning pinkly before looking at her from speculative big green eyes. It miaowed again, as if in question. Oriana slowly reached out and stroked it. She was so tentative, anyone watching her might have thought she was handling the cat as though it were some kind of cleverly disguised bomb, just waiting to explode in her hand.

But in reality, Oriana felt nothing but joy. The cat's fur was warm from the sun; soft and silky and, yes, twitching with pleasure as her soft fingertips feathered lightly across it. The cat began to purr loudly, pushing its head into her hand, wanting more. She scratched the ears, rubbed the cheeks, smoothed the chin, all of which sent the cat into raptures, leaning so far forward into her hand it nearly fell off the wall.

Oriana laughed.

She spent ten minutes fussing the cat, who could have stood it for ten hours. Eventually she forced herself to move on.

8

Some instinct told her it didn't bode well that she should be so delighted by such a simple thing as stroking a cat. In some dark part of her it reminded her of just how bad the last thirteen years had been. And she couldn't afford to think about that.

Not now. Perhaps not ever. So she left the cat, finally finding the brass plaque she was looking for, right at the end of the street. The cat sighed and settled back onto the wall as the human being with such gentle fingers disappeared into the building.

Emma Friels looked at Oriana Foster curiously. 'I'm afraid Mr Bennett doesn't see anybody without an appointment,' she said, for the second time.

When the receptionist had opened the door to Oriana's buzz, and had shown her into the office, Oriana had asked to speak to the senior partner of Bennett, Ride and Contrato, and been informed of this fact. But, instead of leaving, Oriana had simply sat in the nearest chair, neatly placing her bag between her feet. 'I don't mind waiting,' she'd said.

And something about her had suggested to Emma Friels that this young woman could wait, and wait, and wait. A troublemaker then. This had prompted her to repeat, firmly, her statement that nobody at the firm of solicitors saw clients without a prior appointment.

Oriana looked at the secretary now with tired but amused eyes. She smiled. 'I'm sure he'll see me,' she insisted softly.

Well, she was reasonably sure. *If* the anonymous letter hadn't been somebody's idea of a weird joke.

But Oriana didn't think it was. It wasn't easy to arrange for an illicit letter to be smuggled into jail. Most correspondence going through the normal post was subjected to perusal by the prison authorities, even if they denied it. So the fact that somebody had taken the trouble to bribe someone on the inside and arranged for it to reach her meant that they had been very serious indeed.

Of course, she'd disposed of the letter some time ago, not long after receiving it. Every now and then spot checks were performed on prisoners' cells, and although these searches were mostly concerned with finding hidden drugs or makeshift weapons, Oriana wanted to take no chances. Not with a letter such as the one she'd received. If anybody else had read it, and decided to check it out, and it had turned out to be true . . . well, Oriana wasn't sure what might have happened. She only knew she didn't want to risk it. So she'd ripped it to shreds and flushed it down the toilet, but not before every word was ingrained in her memory.

And the name of Mr Christopher Bennett, and this law firm, had been part of that letter. So she sat and smiled at Emma Friels, Christopher Bennett's secretary, and waited.

Emma sighed and got up reluctantly from behind her desk. 'Please wait here,' she said unnecessarily, and walked through. She passed through a small corridor, then tapped discreetly on her boss's door.

Christopher Bennett looked up, surprised at his secretary's appearance at the door. She always used the intercom before coming in, being very well trained.

'Emma?' he said, puzzled. He was a middle-aged man, with newly dyed hair and a smart suit.

Emma firmed her lips. 'I'm sorry, Mr Bennett,' she said – she never called him Christopher, or – worse! – Chris – 'but there's a woman outside who insists on seeing you. She seems to think you'll want to see her when you know her name.' She felt foolish even as she said this. It smacked of something undesirable.

Christopher Bennett frowned. He didn't like the sound of this either. 'Oh. And what is her name?'

Emma grimaced. 'Something rather fanciful, I'm afraid. Oriana. Oriana Foster.'

As she said this name, something remarkable happened to Christopher Bennett's face. It shut down. All expression fled. Only his eyes seemed to glitter.

'Oh,' he said. Then, 'Ah. Yes. You'd . . . er . . . better show her in please, Miss Friels.'

Emma blinked in surprise, then nodded coolly. 'Of course, Mr Bennett,' she said blandly.

Christopher brought the girl's details up on screen, before Emma returned a moment later. 'Miss Foster, sir,' she said.

Oriana walked into an office which was straight out of something on the television. Glass, chrome, leather. Very chic. She glanced straight at the solicitor, however. Unrevealing grey eyes looked back at her.

'Please, sit down,' he said, as his secretary quietly closed the door and walked back to her office, shaking her head.

Christopher looked at Oriana rather like a scientist who had just discovered a new species. She was pale, of course; he'd expected that. Prison pallor, didn't they call it? And she was dressed very plainly, in black skirt and pale yellow pullover, and sneakers without socks. But she was also lovely. Average height, but slender, with tiny wrists and ankles. Sunshine streaming in from outside highlighted her golden curls, but there was nothing little-girlish about her face. High, prominent cheekbones and a firm chin saw to that. And her eyes were magnificent.

But disconcerting.

They were looking back at him as if . . . well, Christopher Bennett wasn't sure. Not cold, exactly. But not friendly. Not hard, but something close. They seemed to challenge him, but at the same time repel him. He was, at heart, a family man, who liked to play golf when he could, go on holiday twice a year, and mow the lawn and clean the cars on a Sunday. This woman, he felt, was so far removed from such a world that she might as well be a leopard.

'Well, what can I . . . er . . . do for you, Miss Foster?' he said. And then felt foolish. Very foolish indeed, for there was obviously only one reason why she could possibly be here.

'I want to know,' Oriana said calmly, her voice cool and yet pleasant, 'if I'm rich.'

Christopher Bennett nodded wisely. 'Oh yes,' he said simply. 'You're rich. In fact, as of this moment, I can confirm you're worth almost two and a half million pounds sterling.'

TWO

Oriana's heart leapt. So it was true! Those wildly unlikely words, written in an illicit letter so long ago, and not even signed, had all been true. She took a long, calming breath.

'I see,' she said at last. And thought that perhaps she really did. If so . . . She was going to have be very careful now. And think very carefully indeed. For a long while, she said nothing further.

Christopher Bennett, aware that someone who'd just been told they were worth millions might well want to take a few moments to sort themselves out, watched and waited. He'd known this day was coming, of course. His client had briefed him fully on what was expected of him. But that had been so many years ago that now it felt as though something had hit him out of the blue.

He looked at Oriana with frank interest. He knew her background, of course. And her story. He supposed it should scare him, but somehow he found it impossible to feel real fear. The young woman in front of him looked almost frail. But there was something in the eyes, perhaps, which made him wonder. Even so, he felt remarkably at ease in her presence.

Oriana stirred at last in her chair and Christopher sat up a little straighter.

'Can you tell me more?' she asked mildly.

The bank account made solely in her name, he informed her, had been in existence since the date of her anonymous letter, and compound interest had added a tidy amount to the original investment of two million. The bank sent him new debit and credit cards for the account every few years, as and when they expired, which he'd be able to dig out for her, along with her PIN, once he'd seen the relevant identification documents.

'And can you tell me who asked you to set up this account for me?' she asked.

'I'm afraid not,' he said firmly.

'Even though the account is in my name?'

'Even so.'

'Would the bank know? Could I find out from them?' she persisted.

'All they could tell you is that I set it up.'

She sighed. 'There's absolutely no way I can persuade you to tell me the name of your client, my mysterious benefactor?'

Christopher shook his head sadly. Oriana nodded. In truth, she'd expected as much. 'I see,' she said again. In some ways it all sounded so dramatic – like something out of Dickens. A poor waif, taken up from poverty and the gutter and offered a new life of wealth and ease by a shadowy figure.

But this wasn't fiction. And Oriana was no Pip.

As Christopher perused her passport and the documents confirming her release, and fetched her debit and credit cards from a wall safe, he wondered what a young woman, just released from jail, would do with so much money. Go wild in the shops, he supposed. Buy up every outfit and pair of shoes, fancy jewellery or flash car which caught her eye. But he was utterly wrong. Oriana hadn't even given a shopping spree a thought. Instead, she was thinking of something else entirely.

'So, you have plans for all that money, hmm?' Christopher probed, a shade condescendingly.

Oriana looked up at him vaguely, obviously having been miles away. But at his words, her eyes focused sharply. 'Oh yes,' she said softly, but something in her voice sent a trickle of unease down the solicitor's back. 'Oh my word yes,' Oriana repeated. 'I have plans all right.'

And her blue eyes glittered.

She left the solicitor's office with the cards securely fastened in the pocket of the holdall. Outside, she took the first taxi she could find to Paddington, and there boarded the next train to Oxford.

* * *

It was raining in the university city, a soft, pleasant rain, which brought out the scent of the late spring flowers and newly mown grass. Oriana booked into the first hotel she came to, a large sprawling place near the station, and after what was probably a rather lacklustre lunch, but which tasted divine compared with the prison fare she was used to, strolled into town.

Her first day out, and here she was, back in her 'home' town, so to speak. The first thing she did was walk to the police station and report in to her parole officer. She then, as per her instructions, signed on at the job centre, although she knew something that the prison authorities didn't. Namely, she wouldn't be needing a job.

Or rather, she thought, as she signed on the dotted line and dutifully perused the 'jobs vacant' cards, she was about to create a job of her own, and thus 'employ' herself.

For that, she'd need a front man.

She scanned the *Oxford Times*, and then the *Oxford Mail*, finding the listings for several independent financial advisers as she did so. She chose one who sounded just about right, a one-man outfit based in Headington, and made an appointment. That done, she walked along St Aldates, and on into the main shopping area of Cornmarket Street. She knew exactly where she was going, even though, over the years, the city centre shops had come and gone, multiplying without her knowledge. But, no matter what, people would always need to buy houses, and so there would always be estate agents.

The first one she saw, nestled next to an entrance to a new shopping mall which hadn't even existed the last time she'd been to the city, was a large go-getting affair, but she passed over the rows of semi-detacheds without so much as a glance. A few old farmhouses were up for sale, but most were upmarket barn conversions in the surrounding villages, a sign of the new times. Oriana ignored them all. She was looking out for one name only: Nether Dene, a village halfway between Oxford and Banbury. The village where she'd been born. The village where her father had lived all his life, before dying in a car crash along with his wife, Oriana's mother, when she was just fifteen.

And then, when at last she spotted it, the name which was forever associated with 'home' in her soul, a photograph of something rather unexpected accompanied it.

Oriana leaned against the window to stop herself from falling. She stared at the picture, mesmerized.

The Manor House was for sale.

The house itself was old, constructed of Cotswold stone, with plenty of windows and an moss-covered roof. It looked run-down. The grounds, what she could see of them in the foreground of the picture, were unkempt. Tiles needed replacing, as did all the window frames. The front door even appeared to be warped. It had, undeniably, the air of a place which had gone to rack and ruin. And, sure enough, when she had gathered herself together enough to read the description, the estate agents themselves cheerfully admitted it was a place with 'potential', a 'fixer-upper' for those with a love of old buildings. Oriana knew what that meant. Apart from anything else, it meant that she could buy the house cheap, because nobody else would want to take it on. Old buildings gobbled up money.

But she was puzzled. And uneasy. As she straightened her shoulders and walked into the estate agent's office, she couldn't help but wonder what had gone wrong. Most of all, she wondered how Lowell Seton could possibly have let the house get so bad. And what catastrophe must have befallen him to make him put his family home up for sale in the first place.

As she thought of Lowell she felt something begin to crack. Something inside her, and out. She felt just like a vase which had a steel band around it, and that band had suddenly threatened to contract. She could feel muscle and tendon, bone and sinew, thought, feeling and imagination, in fact, everything which was herself, give off a warning 'ping'.

Lowell Seton. Just thinking about him could destroy her.

She felt herself faltering inside the doorway. Was she really in any shape to go through with this? But what choice did she have? Desperately, Oriana pushed the thought of Lowell to one side. She would deal with him later. Perhaps, by then, she'd feel less fragile.

As one of the sales staff inside came towards her, unimpressed by her appearance and as yet unaware of the huge shock (and commission) he was about to get from her, Oriana felt a familiar strength come to her aid. It was a strength born of need. Moreover, a strength born of having nothing left to lose. No matter what, Oriana reminded herself, there was no backing out. She'd do whatever it took.

If the Manor House was for sale, so much the better. She wasn't about to look a gift horse in the mouth.

* * *

She slept fitfully that night. Perhaps it was because the usual chorus of clanging doors, locks turning in their keyholes, women calling to one another and heavy feet pounding ponderously along steel flooring had been replaced by the more whimsical sounds of a provincial hotel.

Traffic. Guests coming in late from the bar. Old plumbing creaking and gurgling. Oriana sighed, and buried her head in the pillow.

When dawn came she was already awake to meet it, and was one of the first down to breakfast. Presented with a choice which went beyond cornflakes, she opted for some Greek yoghurt and apricots, and had two pots of coffee. She sat at a table by the window, smiling as a sparrow outside on the pavement fought with a starling for a discarded crumb. She was, she realized with a satisfied sigh, beginning to feel human again. And yet, as she watched her fellow guests, a curious mixture of travelling executive types, tourists and conference-goers, she knew she would always be somewhat different, or set apart from the rest of humanity. It was something only another such as herself would ever be able to understand.

Telling herself to look forward, not back, Oriana left the hotel and walked into town. Soon, she'd have to buy some decent clothes, but that could wait. This afternoon she had an appointment with her front man. She knew he'd probably try to thrust his business prowess on to her, especially once he got a glimmer of her personal fortune, but Oriana wasn't about to invest in stocks and bonds, or in any way tie up her money.

She knew exactly what she wanted to do with it. And since she'd already entered into negotiations to buy the Manor House at Nether Dene, and was determined to have it safely in her hands as soon as possible, she'd very quickly need the services of a good front man, someone who knew how to put up a corporate front, and hide her own identity behind it.

Soon, she was sure, she was going to need all the protection such anonymity could give her. And thinking of protection . . .

Oriana slowly came to a halt as she considered this problem. She had just reached Carfax, and all around her other people were also standing around waiting, but for them it was a matter of waiting for the famous Carfax clock to strike, and for the mechanical figures to come out into the open. But Oriana was blind to the tourist delights of her home town.

Instead, she was thinking hard. For it was true — she was going to need protection. And of a particular sort.

Nodding to herself, she made for the nearest phone booth and consulted the Yellow Pages. Leafing through, she could see one of them was situated just around the corner, so she set off with purpose.

* * *

Connor O'Dell got to the office early that morning. He parked his car as usual, in South Parks Road, and walked towards the High Street, where his office was situated on the second floor of an old, one-time butcher's shop overlooking the covered market. Now he owned the whole building, and as he walked up the front steps he glanced, as always, at the discreet sign on the well-scrubbed wall. 'O'Dell Security' was all it said. To the many clients who used its services, it needed no other inducements or explanations.

He walked into reception, raising a cheerful hand in greeting to Marion, the telephonist, and carried on up the stairs. Up here were the offices of his three full-time assistants: Mike Grant, the computer expert, who was always in demand, especially when it came to clients nervous of hackers and wanting the best anti-theft programmes created and installed on their company computers; Geoff Burlington, an ex-copper and something of a surveillance expert, who usually got the flat-foot, painstaking work which came with industrial espionage; and Yassim Abdullah, who spoke more languages than Connor could guess at, and had more friends in foreign places than he would even try to imagine.

At the moment, the rotund, friendly-faced linguist was abroad, working on a case for a large oil corporation. Connor was expecting a nice big fat payment soon.

He walked into his own office, which was spacious and comfortable, and went straight to his desk. A tall man at just over six feet five, he had the broad, muscular build of the ex-soldier that he was. He shrugged off his jacket straight away and loosened his tie and cuffs before sitting down in a heavy leather chair and attacking the pile of mail his secretary, Julie, had left ready for him.

He was busy sorting through it when Julie buzzed him.

'Hi, boss,' she said cheerfully. 'You ready for some walk-in business? Marion says there's a client downstairs.'

Connor pressed the button on the intercom. 'Sure. Show him up.' He was a little surprised. O'Dell Security didn't, as a rule, get much 'street' custom. Most of their work came as a result of word of mouth within the business community, or personal contacts cultivated over the years by his assistants. He hoped, whoever the potential client was, he hadn't mistaken O'Dell's for a private investigator's office. They didn't do divorces.

Julie appeared at the door a moment later and coughed. The cough was a dead giveaway. She only ever coughed when she was puzzled, wrong-footed, or downright worried.

'Miss Foster, Mr O'Dell,' she said, and stepped aside. And Connor could instantly see why Julie was coughing. The young woman who walked in, dressed in clothes which his sister wouldn't even bother to give away to a jumble sale, wasn't the kind of client O'Dell was used to.

'Thank you for seeing me at such short notice,' Oriana said, something in her voice, a cool kind of awareness, instantly making Connor rethink his first impression. With her curly blonde hair, big blue eyes and Little Orphan Annie outfit, Connor thought that anyone could be mistaken for totally misreading Miss Foster. The voice, however, if you were as aware of human nature and as experienced in its nuances as Connor O'Dell undoubtedly was, was more than enough to make you think again.

'That's quite all right,' Connor said pleasantly, but definitely noncommittally.

Oriana detected his aloofness, and understood it. She'd heard many such a voice in prison. It was the voice of experience, of someone who knew the ropes; a person whose advice you listened to and who you made a mental note never to cross.

Something of her understanding reached him, elevating her yet more in his esteem, and he paused in the act of holding out a chair. Then the moment passed and he stood back to allow her to sit. He glanced at Julie.

'Geoff says he needs to take on some more temporary staff for the night watchmen's outfit in Didcot,' Julie said, giving him the opening to cut the interview short, should he need it. He nodded, but said nothing, and after a moment Julie withdrew. When he took his own seat, it was to find Miss Foster looking at him with gently amused, knowing eyes.

She had no illusions about the kind of picture she presented, and Connor O'Dell's reaction to her, far from making her angry or resentful, made her feel almost mellow. For now she was sure that she'd come to the right place. Nothing and nobody got past this man, of that she was utterly convinced.

Connor noticed that she had no handbag, and that she was wearing no make-up. It accentuated her paleness.

Oriana let him watch her for a moment, and then she said, 'Mr O'Dell, do you do bodyguard work in this firm?'

Connor slowly leaned back in his chair. 'Not so often nowadays,' he said slowly. And truthfully.

But when he'd first started in this job, after leaving the army with an honourable discharge and his life savings, he'd been the sole employee of the newly created O'Dell Security, and a large part of his early work *had* included that of personal bodyguard. His martial arts training, courtesy of the SAS, had special appeal to certain clients, especially those in the entertainment business. But since he'd gradually taken on more partners, and slowly but inexorably expanded the range of the firm's activities and specialities, the bodyguard work had been all but phased out.

'But you do still provide such services?' Oriana persisted.

Connor looked at her wide blue eyes thoughtfully. Now why did a girl like this need a bodyguard?

'Are you rich then, Miss Foster?' he asked softly, his green eyes looking out from a craggily handsome face with no hint of flirtatiousness or even apparent curiosity.

Oriana smiled slightly. 'Oh yes,' she said simply.

Connor quickly ran his eyes over her clothes, took in the old jeans and battered sneakers and went back to her face. Hardly the usual attire of a wealthy woman. Perhaps she was a bit eccentric, although her manner didn't suggest it. It didn't strike him that Miss Foster was lying to him about the money either. Connor knew when he was being lied to. And when he wasn't.

Oriana could almost hear the cogs turning in his head. Not that his craggy face gave away a single thought. A stray shaft of sunlight, escaping from a rather cloudy sky, shone briefly through the window and illuminated his dark blond hair, cut casually and slightly long.

Oriana waited. She could wait all day. Connor, looking at her, sitting so economically relaxed in the chair, knew and understood that kind of patience. And where it was bred. One end of his wide, generous mouth quirked upwards. 'Miss Foster,' he said softly, 'have you been in prison?'

'I got out yesterday,' Oriana confirmed frankly.

'And you feel in need of a bodyguard already?'

Oriana grinned. She couldn't help it. She liked Connor O'Dell. 'I do. Or rather, to be more accurate,' she said, being scrupulously honest, 'I believe I *will* have need of one. Soon.'

Connor nodded. It was a fine distinction, that. A significant one too. 'And do you have any idea how long you'll need a bodyguard for?' He was intrigued. It had been some years since he'd been in the field himself; as of late, office work seemed to take precedence over everything. And with Yassim away, and Geoff and Mike having everything under control in their own areas, he was aware that if he wanted to take a break from the office, now was as good a time as any.

Besides, Miss Foster interested him.

'Not more than three months, I think, from the beginning of next week,' she said crisply.

'You sound quite definite about that,' he said, for the first time taken aback.

Oriana shrugged, thought about it, then held out her hand and waggled it side to side in a telling gesture. 'So so,' she amended. In fact, she was pretty sure that if she hadn't done what she intended to do in three months, she was never going to do it at all.

'Do you have any specific ideas about the threat which faces you?' Connor asked.

Oriana paused and thought for a moment. 'I just need someone to be with me, twenty-four hours a day, to keep an eye on me. Someone who knows how to handle himself. What's more, I'll know, or probably have a good idea, when things might start to get a little . . . fraught.'

'You're saying you think that someone, at some point, will try to harm you?' he translated bluntly.

Oriana thought about it, and Connor watched her like a hawk. She didn't look particularly alarmed. Nor did she look like the kind of neurotic who lived in some kind of drama of their own making. No, he had no doubts that Miss Foster was serious.

'I think it's possible that someone might try and kill me,' Oriana said at last, sounding perfectly calm and matter-of-fact.

'I see. In that case I think I can help you,' he said.

Oriana looked at him levelly. 'You're thinking of taking on the job yourself?'

Connor nodded, unsurprised by the fact that she'd been able to read him so easily. 'Do you want to hear my credentials?'

'No, it's fine,' she said. 'I trust you're more than capable.'

'Will you want me to live in?'

Oriana nodded. 'Yes. But it will be in a big house, so there'll be no problem about room.'

'You'll want the place made secure?'

Oriana nodded. 'Yes, to a certain extent. But you won't need to go overboard.' She paused, wondering how to phrase this next bit delicately. Connor, sensing her reluctance, raised one shaggy eyebrow in encouragement. Oriana took a deep breath. There was no easy way to ask, she supposed. She'd just have to blurt it out. 'I was rather hoping that your, er, profession not be obvious. That is, I'm hoping to pass you off as . . .' she paused, searching for the right word.

'Your boyfriend?' Connor helped her out. It was, after all, the obvious cover.

Oriana nodded. 'Exactly. My boyfriend. The protective kind, naturally.'

Connor smiled. 'Naturally,' he repeated, then got down to business, discussing fees and drawing up a contract. Once Oriana had signed Connor paused and looked up at her.

'There is just one thing I want to know,' he said quietly, 'before I sign this.'

Oriana tensed. For she knew what that 'one thing' was bound to be. She looked at him with clear, level blue eyes. 'You want to know what I served time for,' she hazarded coolly.

Connor nodded.

Oriana looked at him.

'Murder,' she said calmly.

* * *

Lowell Seton turned off the main road and took the narrow, winding lane into Nether Dene. He passed the cricket pitch, where some schoolboys were practising, then drove the Range Rover down the even narrower lane which led to the church, a huge sprawling vicarage, and the Manor and Dower Houses.

As he drove past the laurel-bedecked entranceway to the Manor he caught a flash of red in the hedge, and quickly touched the brakes. Sure enough, the 'For Sale' notice had a big triumphant 'Sold' splashed across it.

He cursed under his breath. Just when he'd almost scraped together enough to buy the house, it went off the market. 'Damn!' he muttered.

He was still cursing his luck as he drove on and, a few hundred yards further on down the lane, turned into the entrance of the Dower House Hotel.

The Dower House, as its name implied, had been built by the original owner of the Manor House back in the 1700s to accommodate his mother. It was a huge house in its own right, and ten years ago Lowell had turned it into a classic country house hotel, with room for a dozen guests. With the River Cherwell nearby, as well as the Oxford Canal, it was a regular and popular spot with anglers, as well as tourists wanting a base within easy reach of Oxford, Stratford-upon-Avon, and, of course, London itself.

He parked near the entrance, looking up as an old Rolls-Royce, circa 1942, pulled up. A chauffeur, clad in navy blue with all the trimmings, climbed out and opened the back door. Two beaming American ladies stepped out.

'Thank you, James,' one gushed, as the chauffeur helped her out of the stately vehicle.

James Brent was one of Lowell's employees, and along with two others, drove the fleet of classic cars which Lowell had had revamped and turned into a secondary business. Now Seton Cars hired out a range of luxury vehicles, such as the Rolls, a Morgan, an Aston Martin, and a Lagonda, offering a champagne and strawberry tour of the Cotswolds to any Dower House Hotel guest who cared to fork out the money for it. Weddings were still, however, its main source of income.

Lowell turned and went in through a side entrance, but his presence hadn't gone unnoticed by the two American ladies, who were rather taken with the hotel owner. At just over six feet, and with jet-black hair, cool grey eyes and the kind of classically handsome, lord-of-the-manor features which they'd seen in British television series, Lowell made many a female heart flutter.

Right now, he walked into his office, closed the door, and sat at his desk gloomily. He ran a hand through his black hair, staring blankly at the wall opposite him. An oil painting, old and in need of cleaning, stared back at him.

Why did the Manor House have to be sold now, when it had already been on the market for over six months? He'd made a promise to his mother before she died that he'd do everything in his power to get back the old family home and dammit – he slammed his clenched fist on the desk– he'd do just that. Perhaps he could make an offer to the new owners.

He reached for the phone to call the estate agent, but they'd already left for the day. He sighed and walked to the window which overlooked the river and the lush water-meadows beyond it. A guest, carrying a golf bag, plodded his way to his car.

Lowell was an elegant figure, in a dark suit and plain gold cufflinks. He leaned forward on the windowsill, and sighed heavily. He wasn't sure why, but he'd been feeling what his grandmother would have called 'fey' all day. He'd been restless, sensing that some kind of a storm was brewing. But the storm wasn't in the sky, it was lurking somewhere on a more personal plane. Whatever it was, he hoped it would arrive soon. Never one to flinch from a challenge, he nonetheless hated this grim, tense feeling. Perhaps it had something to do with the Manor apparently having slipped through his fingers at the eleventh hour. Whatever it was, he had no doubts at all about his ability to overcome whatever it was that threatened him.

He *would* have been astonished, however, to learn that the name of his personal tempest was Oriana Foster. And that the onslaught was about to rain down right over his head.

With a vengeance.

THREE

Mercedes Seton looked down at the wriggling pup in her arms and smiled as it strained its thick neck upwards to try and lick her face. Beside her, a well-padded woman in a light summer raincoat watched and also smiled. Next to her, a teenaged boy stared at the dog with eager eyes.

'I think you'll find that this one is just the chap you're looking for, Mrs Frobisher,' Mercedes said. 'His sire was best in breed at Crufts three years ago. He'll be a big boy though – just look at those paws!'

The boy beamed, obviously delighted with the thought of owning a big dog. The boxer puppy yelped, seeming as eager as the boy to get off to his new home and start playing. Mrs Frobisher laughed. 'I dare say we can afford to keep him in chump steak. Just! Well, Wes, what do you think?'

'He's great,' her son said, as if there could be any doubt. Sensing a new acolyte, the pup was already trying to leap from Mercedes' arms and into the boy's, and she willingly handed the pup over. Boy and dog went into mutual raptures.

'Now, he's had all his shots so far,' Mercedes said, getting down to the serious business and fixing her latest client with a stern eye. 'His parvo virus, plus his first worming. I have flea treatment here.' She indicated a bag of 'goodies' which she gave away with every pup she sold. 'Do you have a vet in mind?' she asked, although Mercedes already knew that Mrs Frobisher had kept a Yorkshire terrier for over fifteen years. She always checked out her clients for suitability before agreeing to sell any of her dogs.

'Oh yes.' Mrs Frobisher named a local vet, and Mercedes nodded.

'Can we call him Spike, Mum?' Wes piped up, and Mrs Frobisher scowled.

'No, we can't,' she said firmly.

'Oh, Mum. He looks like a Spike,' her son whined, and Mercedes grinned as she followed the still amicably bickering pair outside to their car. Waving them off, the puppy too busy licking its new master's face to even give her a passing thought, Mercedes sighed happily and turned back through her gate. Ahead of her was a small but attractive stone cottage. As she walked up the slightly uneven path, her eye moved from side to side, looking over the cottage garden with a knowing eye. She exclaimed at the sight of a familiar star-shaped pattern of leaves, and reached down to uproot the dandelion before it could flower. Beside her, fat ginger-coloured bees droned in the lavender which bordered the small diamond-shaped flower bed.

Back in the cottage, she went to the kitchen to make a cup of tea, looking out over the kennels which sprawled over most of the back garden. The female boxer who'd just lost one of her brood stretched lazily in her spot under a shady laburnum tree. She still had two pups with her, but they were due to leave next week. In a separate kennel and dog run, her mate watched her placidly.

Mercedes had three breeding pairs of boxers, and she was about to show one of them, a three-year-old, at a local prestigious show. Soon, she'd have to get the grooming gear out, but not just yet.

She made herself a cup of tea, taking it into the small living room which looked out at the Dower House, now her brother's hotel, and, a little further on, the more imposing edifice which was the Manor. She'd grown up in that huge house, as blissful as any tomboy could be with her own apple orchard, a nearby river, and more trees to climb than you could shake a stick at.

After a leisurely read of the local paper, she gathered her leashes to 'saddle up the boys', as she always thought of it. She walked them in relays, usually in groups of three. As usual, the fearsome-looking dogs displayed their soft-as-butter natures as she approached, stumpy tails wagging the whole of their rear ends as she fussed them and slipped on the leads.

They were used to this routine, and immediately fell into position: one on her left, two on her right. None pulled on the leash, all waited and sat at the kerb whenever she was about to cross the road, and none of them was aggressive with other dogs. She did her own dog training and ran occasional classes, whenever her income looked like it was falling off, or she needed a little extra spending money.

Mercedes closed the white picket gate carefully behind her as she went out, crossing the road and automatically taking the footpath past the church. There she checked on her parents' grave, noting that the wallflowers were wilting, and made a mental note to bring some fresh flowers from the garden tomorrow. The white peonies were due out, and always lasted longer than the red ones – plus they had a nice scent. Mix them with some lovely powder-blue love-in-a-mist and some orange japonica, and she'd have a nice arrangement.

She moved on through the lopsided stones, over the stile in the wall and on to the unofficial footpath which took her through the rear garden of the old Manor, which was now so overgrown only the locals kept up a path through it, being as it was a popular shortcut on the way to the river and canal.

She was just pushing aside a huge glossy laurel when the dog on her right suddenly growled. It was so unusual for any of her dogs to growl that she stopped dead in her tracks.

'Sorry, did I scare her?' a voice asked, coming from the seemingly impenetrable thicket of bushes just beside her.

Then they parted, and Mercedes wondered how it was ever possible that she could have missed him, for the man emerging in front of her was huge. Tall as a house, and seemingly built like one. But, as he emerged into the May sunshine, the light caught his shaggy blond hair, and one side of his craggy face, and Mercedes' breath hitched as green eyes twinkled down at her.

At five feet ten herself, Mercedes wasn't used to having men loom so very far above her, but she found herself rather liking it. She liked, even more, the cool mint-green eyes which looked back at her.

Connor slowly reached down to let the boxer nearest to him smell his hand, but there was nothing to worry about. As he knew, they were friendly animals, and she'd only growled in the first place because he'd taken her by surprise. Now she slobbered all over his outstretched palm, making him grin.

Connor had been looking over his new 'digs' with an eye to security. The Manor itself was a well-built edifice, but the grounds were a maze of broken-down walls, sagging fences and wide-open areas. A nightmare to secure, in other words. It was a good thing Oriana didn't need it to be a fortress. As it was, he'd been prowling the grounds looking to set up one or two alarms in strategic places – nothing fancy or high tech, but enough to give him any warning if they had trespassers.

He'd hardly needed his army training, however, to spot the woman walker and her three dogs long before they were anywhere near him, but he'd been cautious enough to just check her out. Obviously, though, she was local, and by the looks of it, this part of the Manor grounds was a free-for-all for anybody. He'd have to ask Oriana if she wanted this unofficial right-of-way blocked off. He doubted it would make her popular if she did, but it would certainly make his job easier.

Now he reached down and roughhoused with the dogs, who were big enough to enjoy such ungentle petting. Mercedes watched, with dog-lover's approval, as he introduced himself to her charges.

'They're in fine fettle,' Connor said, straightening up once more, and looking down at the lady. With long black hair tied back in a simple ponytail, and large hazel eyes, she was very easy to look at. In fact, he felt he could look at her all day.

Mercedes felt a small fire light deep inside her. He was interested in her. She knew that at once. And she was interested in him. It had been over a year since she'd had a lover, and that had ended rather acrimoniously. Jake had wanted to get married, but she had known it would never work. He'd taken her refusal as a rejection, which it hadn't been, but things had gone downhill from there. Now, her body was letting her know in no uncertain terms that perhaps the time for celibacy was past.

She stirred briefly, not because she felt uncomfortable under those pale green eyes which seemed to see everything, but because she wondered if he could sense her own arousal. She smiled. 'Are you lost?' she asked. It wasn't unusual for one of the guests at the hotel to wander off, en route to the village pub or the tow path.

Connor smiled. 'Not yet,' he said softly. 'But is that a hint that you want me to? Get lost, I mean?'

Mercedes laughed. She liked a man with a sense of humour. Moreover, she liked one who had confidence in himself. For she would have bet her last pound coin that this man knew damned well that 'getting lost' was the last thing she wanted him to do.

'No,' she said firmly. 'But my brother owns the hotel, and I consider it an unofficial duty of mine to shepherd any lost sheep back his way.'

Connor realized that she thought he was a tourist, opened his mouth to tell her that he wasn't, that he was living at the Manor, then abruptly closed it again. Because, of course, he was supposed to be the live-in boyfriend of Oriana Foster. But he didn't want to say as much to this woman. It was stupid, of course. She was obviously local, and was bound to find out sooner or later. But he didn't want to spoil the moment. It wasn't often that two strangers felt an instant spark like this.

Normally, Connor would have followed up such an occurrence like a shot. He hadn't reached the age of thirty-one without knowing how special and rare these opportunities were. As a young man, and a soldier at that, he'd had his share of casual flings, one-night stands, even, once, a shot at something more permanent. But it felt as if he already knew this woman. Or at least, looking down into her frank hazel eyes, he felt as if he *would* know this woman.

In every meaning of the word.

Mercedes, looking back at him, was thinking much along the same lines, and, if she'd been able to read minds, would have found herself nodding in agreement.

There was something plain and simple and right about this moment. Something natural. She'd see him again. They'd learn about one another. They'd make love. And maybe, maybe, if the spark was enough, and turned into the right kind of flame, the kind which could become a permanent, warming, sustaining fire . . . well then, who knows? She smiled. As she did so, Connor heard a door open in the Manor House behind him. Oriana must have arrived.

'Well, I'll see you around, I hope,' Connor said quickly. He reached down to pat the boxers, then nodded and went away. But not without regret.

It wasn't until he was out of sight that Mercedes realized that, for all his size and bulk, she hadn't heard him crashing through the undergrowth. What an unusual man. And talk about sexy! She caught the eye of her female boxer, and grinned at her scrunched-up face.

'Wow, Beattie,' she said softly. 'You don't meet one of those every day of the week!'

Her phone rang at just gone four that afternoon. She got to it just in time, as she'd been bathing her potential show dog in a special shampoo that cost the earth. Naturally, no self-respecting dog wanted to be caught dead smelling of it, and the usual result had followed – namely, Mercedes ended up wetter than her canine companion.

31

She wiped some foam off the end of her nose as she picked up the receiver. 'Yes?'

'Hello, Sis. One of the waiters tells me that the chef is in a cooking mood. Want to come over for dinner?'

At the sound of her brother's voice, she sat down in her chair, smiling. 'Sure. Why not?' The hotel chef was renowned for his food, but sometimes he outdid himself. The people who worked with him had learned to recognize these times and pass the news on. And, as if by magic, the hotel's restaurant was always full on such nights. How the locals, and some not-so-locals got to hear about it, Mercedes still hadn't figured out. But, like everyone else, she was more than happy to take advantage of the phenomenon whenever it occurred.

'In fact, why not come over for tea? They're about to serve it,' Lowell said.

'OK. I'll be there in five minutes. But none of that cream-tea stuff,' she warned. The Dower House Hotel was famous for its cream teas, and attracted tourists from miles around. But if she was to save herself for Henri's offerings tonight, the scones, clotted cream and wild strawberry preserves would just have to be sacrificed.

* * *

Lowell was in his study-cum-office when his sister walked in. She was humming, something she didn't often do, and he wondered what had put her in such a good mood. He eyed her damp jeans and blouse, and sniffed knowingly. 'You have a show coming up?'

Mercedes nodded. 'The weekend.'

Lowell looked up as Maureen, one of the kitchen staff, came in with a tea tray. He smiled and thanked her, failing to notice the lingering glance she gave him on the way out. Mercedes noticed it though, and smiled. Lowell would have to watch out for that one. But then, her brother always had to watch out for women. He was a magnet for them.

At the moment, he was dressed in a white shirt and black slacks, his tie and jacket having long since been discarded. On Lowell, the family's raven-black hair was shaped by an expensive hairdresser into a style which totally suited his square, almost too-handsome face, being generously layered on top, and tapering to a duck's tail at the back.

Growing up with Lowell as her brother had been something of a trial for Mercedes, since all her friends wheedled and whined for her to take them to her home to hang out, just so that they could catch a glimpse of him. Never Rollo. Just Lowell. Her brother, the heart-throb of Nether Dene. Not to mention the surrounding five counties. She grinned in remembrance. And how often had he, a lofty four minutes older than herself, ever deigned to notice their existence? More often than not, Mercedes was left to pick up the pieces and play the unwanted role of agony aunt.

She'd lost count of how many friends had mysteriously fallen away after their interest was unrequited. In fact, Mercedes had only had one friend, her best friend in fact, who never— But no. Even before she could finish the thought, Mercedes shut it down. It was automatic. She did it almost without realising.

'So, did you notice the house has been sold?' Lowell asked, for Mercedes had been away for a few days, looking at a couple of dogs on the east coast, and had only recently returned.

'No! You've finally bought it!' Mercedes cried, her face lighting up, because she knew how much it meant to him. Ever since they'd lost the Manor, and their mother had been so bitter, Lowell had striven to get it back. Turning the Dower House into a hotel, revamping the family collection of classic cars and turning them into a lucrative side-shoot, his courting of bankers, of saving every penny, of studiously studying the stock and money markets to boost his capital — it had all been done with the ultimate goal of getting back the Manor.

For herself, she'd been quite happy to move into the estate's single cottage, but her mother had hated it there.

Lowell, of course, had overseen the conversion of the Dower House and had a small suite on the top floor. But her smile fell as he shot her a grim look, then shook his head. Mercedes bit her lip. 'But I thought you said you were finally, more or less, able to come up with the asking price?' she said softly.

Lowell laughed. It was a hard, bitter laugh, and it made his sister wince. She literally couldn't remember the last time she'd heard her brother laugh as if he meant it. Couldn't remember, in fact, ever seeing him happy. Not for years. Not since . . . Again, the automatic shutdown. Mercedes instantly moved on to something else.

'Didn't you say you might even take out a bridging loan?' she queried.

'Yes,' Lowell said shortly. 'I was going to put in an application next month. Then I noticed the Sold sign had gone up. Can you bloody believe it?' he snarled.

Mercedes shook her head. But, in truth, she felt strangely relieved. 'You know,' she said tentatively, 'it was always *Mother's* dream to get the Manor back,' she said. 'But Mum's been dead for over two years now, Lowell. Don't you think this might be a sign? You know, perhaps somebody telling you that it's time to move on? After all, you've got the hotel, and the cars. You're nearly a millionaire in your own right. Do you really need to have such a big house hung around your neck now, like an albatross?'

Lowell, who'd been pouring the tea, looked up at her slowly. He was surprised. But not, she thought with a surge of hope, particularly hurt.

'I don't think of it as an albatross,' Lowell said flatly. 'I consider it our family home. And we should never have lost it.'

Mercedes looked away. She didn't want to talk about that. She never wanted to talk about that. 'Yes, Lowell, but Mum and Dad are gone.' And Rollo is gone, she thought, but of course didn't say aloud. 'It's only you and me now, and I have the cottage. Is it really so important that you get the Manor back? How will you refurbish it? You know yourself the kitchen floor needs totally redoing. As does the east part of the roof. Then there's the damp, new plumbing . . . Is it worth it?'

Lowell leaned back in his chair. He looked tired, wearily, hopelessly tired. Mercedes wished she could wipe that look away, but it seemed to be almost a part of him now. Sometimes it scared her. She'd thought, for a while, that perhaps Margaret could take that dark, brooding air of unhappiness from him, and replace it with something better. Now she was not so sure.

Oh, they seemed to get on all right. They'd been together for nearly four years now. They seemed to fit, in an odd sort of way. And, even though it made her feel slightly ashamed to think it, Margaret was so wealthy, she'd probably make the perfect wife for Lowell. And Mercedes knew that Margaret readily saw herself as 'Lady of the Manor'. In fact, Mercedes sometimes wondered why she didn't pop the question herself, since Lowell seemed remarkably reluctant to do so.

'I grew up there, Mercy,' Lowell said, using her childhood nickname. 'I want my kids to do the same. Nowadays it's all computers and instant this, instant that. Kids don't have what you and I had in that house. The old nursery, where generations of Setons grew up, names carved in the woodwork going back to 1699. Remember finding that one in the kitchen pantry?'

Mercedes did. 'Going to school just up the road,' she mused, 'where Dad had gone before us, and Granddad. Yes, I know what you mean, Lowell. But you still have the Dower House.'

'The Dower House is a hotel, Mercy, not a home,' Lowell said flatly. 'Anyway, I've been on to the estate agents. They're being cagey. They say the new owners don't want their details bandied about. Now what's that supposed to mean? What's the big secret?' He shifted uneasily in his chair, his dove-grey eyes hardening. 'I dare say they're property developers, and are going to turn the Manor into flats,' he said bitterly. 'I can just see it now. Delightful des reses for the new upwardly mobile. Ideal weekend places for the stressed-out executive. A charming retirement pad for well-heeled OAPs. It makes me sick.'

Mercedes sighed heavily. 'I'm sorry, Lowell,' she said helplessly. But what could she do? She had no money.

Lowell sighed. 'It's not your problem. Don't worry – I'll sort it out.'

And he probably would, too, Mercedes thought grimly. And perhaps therein lay all the trouble. For, as the younger son, Lowell had been raised with all the freedom of someone who'd never been expected to have to carry the burden of one day being head of the household, to retain the family estates and keep the money flowing.

So when, so cruelly, so unexpectedly, and so tragically, he'd become just that, Lowell hadn't been prepared. Or rather, he *thought* that he hadn't been prepared. To Mercedes and their mother, however, Lowell had always been the strong one. Cleverer than Rollo, he'd read economics at Oxford. More forward-thinking than their father, who'd died when Mercedes was eighteen, he'd steered the Seton family from near ruin to respected hoteliers. Lowell had never faltered, whereas Mercedes, for two long years, had buried her head in the sand like some human ostrich and refused to come out. Their mother, especially, had relied on him with unflagging dependence, and he'd never let her down.

So why did he see himself as such a failure? Why, in spite of having one of the richest and most sought-after women around hot and hungry to marry him, why, when he'd become such a successful businessman and all-round decent human being, was her brother so unhappy? So tormented?

She couldn't understand it. Or rather, she could. She just didn't want to think about it.

* * *

Margaret Wright put the final touch of lipstick to her mouth, and leaned back in the mirror to survey her reflection. She didn't look forty-two. In fact, she didn't look thirty-two. The plastic surgeon in Switzerland last year had been worth every last penny.

She put on her Ralph Lauren jacket, which perfectly matched her tailored trousers and knee-high, Italian-made boots, and fluffed out her platinum blonde hair. She wanted to look especially good tonight. Lowell was taking her to a new place in Stratford.

Perhaps tonight was the night.

She tripped gaily down the stairs and went to the library, looking in on her father, Fred Wright, the so-called Supermarket King. He didn't much look like the man who owned a supermarket in nearly every town for a 150-mile radius. He looked old and fluffy. Her dear old man. An only child, Margaret was used to being the apple of his eye. Hadn't she divorced her first husband because Fred hadn't approved?

'Hello, Pops, I'm just off,' she said, waking him up unrepentantly from his doze. He was doing that a lot lately – dozing off. He was losing weight too. But it was about time that he lost the podge, she thought.

Fred Wright woke with a start, blinked, and eyed his daughter knowingly. 'Lowell?' he asked gruffly.

Margaret laughed. 'Of course Lowell,' she said. At twenty-nine, Lowell Seton was almost fourteen years her junior. But nowadays, who counted? Surely her grumpy old bear didn't really object to Lowell's age? 'I'll be back late, don't wait up,' she said. As if he would.

Fred frowned. 'Margie,' he said warningly, but she turned quickly and stared at him. Something in her dark-brown eyes withered the words on his lips. Instead, he shook his head helplessly. He was feeling more and more helpless nowadays. And scared. Margaret scared him. Twice married, twice divorced. And now this thing with Lowell. With *Lowell Seton*, of all men. What was she playing at? Why was she doing it? He didn't understand.

Something of his weary puzzlement must have registered with his daughter, for she smiled, sighed theatrically, then came over and kissed the top of his balding head. 'Brush up the old wedding suit, Pops,' she said cheerfully, as she turned on her smartly made heels and headed for the door. 'Something tells me we're going to be celebrating an engagement soon.'

Margaret had never had a better lover than Lowell. Or a better-looking one. Or one who came attached to a family line which went back further than a genealogist was able to trace. He was perfect. What's more, he desperately wanted to get his Manor back. And Margaret, with all her vast fortune, could help him get it. But so far, he'd been reluctant to propose. But Margaret was working on it. And what little Margie Wright wanted, little Margie got.

In the hallway she paused to inspect her perfectly proportioned, petite five-foot one-inch figure, and nodded. Her waist would make a wasp envious.

Fred watched her go, his hands fretfully pulling a newspaper into little pieces.

* * *

Back in Nether Dene, Lowell glanced at his watch. He was late. He'd taken a walk along the towpath after his tea with Mercedes, only at the last-minute remembering that he had a prior engagement with Margaret. He'd left Mercedes in his den, amused but promising to take dinner in the restaurant without him, and went up to change. But the same restlessness which had been plaguing him for days now made him seek a brisk walk outside to help clear his head. The birds were busy nesting, and some moorhens even had youngsters, tiny black balls of fluff which floated on the canal like corks, but he'd been blind to the beauty of nature.

He walked fast and hard now, a handsome figure in a dark suit. He took the shortcut through the back of the Manor, too polite to keep Margaret waiting. So he had his head down, his mind wrapped up in other things, and simply wasn't watching where he was going.

Oriana had no such excuse.

When she'd gone into the garden to cut some greenery for a flower arrangement, determined to enjoy every new-found scrap of freedom – including the simple pleasure of having fresh cut flowers in the house – she'd heard someone approaching her long before she could see who it was. Expecting a villager and knowing that, sooner or later, she'd have to make her presence known, and weather the shock and backlash it would bring, she made no effort to hide. Had she known who was coming, however, she would have done just that.

But then, when she saw him, his dark head bent as he moved swiftly towards her with that lithe, feline grace of his which was so familiar, she simply couldn't move. Not even to save her life. She felt literally rooted to the ground. Her throat went dry, so dry she couldn't even make a sound to alert him.

Lowell.

Panic hit her. Longing. Pain. Sweetness. More Panic.

Lowell, some instinct at last alerting him to the fact that he was no longer alone, looked up. At first, all he saw was a blonde woman, standing on a patch of overgrown lawn, holding a trug full of green sprays and white laurel flowers.

Then their eyes met, and his world stopped turning. And he knew. He went white. Bone white.

'*You*,' he whispered.

FOUR

Connor rinsed out his coffee mug and set it aside on the draining board. As he did so, he looked up out of the Manor's rather grimy kitchen window, and swore.

Hard.

Outside, Oriana stood facing a man. And, even from this distance, he could sense the tension in the air. He was at the door less than a second later. Perhaps he was getting too damned old for this kind of assignment. Losing his edge. He should never have let her out of his sight. He moved fast but silently out of the door, automatically keeping to cover. Not that he needed to bother. Neither Oriana nor Lowell would have been aware of his existence if he'd come bellowing outside like a bull.

As he approached, Connor got a better look at the stranger and, for a moment, his step faltered. He recognized that look. It was the look of a man suddenly thrust into his own personal hell.

Oriana was thinking much the same thing, and her heart was aching so hard she almost felt sure she was having a heart attack, because she knew it was due to her. He was so pale. His eyes, usually the soft grey-blue of a dove's wing, seemed to be darkening, deepening, as if some darkness in his soul was leaching into his eyes.

Darkness which *she* had put there.

She took a breath, and tried not to faint. She'd known this moment would be tough. Had always known, throughout the long thirteen years that she'd been inside, that this was the one moment, the only thing, that might possibly persuade her not to come back to Nether Dene at all. To see, to have to endure, this look on his face. But she'd convinced herself she could stand it. Fool. How had she ever thought that she could bear the man she loved to look at her as if . . . as if . . .

Lowell took a long, shuddering breath. Connor was now only a yard away, but he knew that neither of them had seen him. Instinct made him wait. But if the other man made one move towards her . . .

'Hello, Lowell,' Oriana heard herself say. And was as astonished to hear it as Lowell seemed to be. Could that calm, clear voice really be coming from her? Could anything that normal come from someone who felt on the verge of madness or death or utter despair?

Lowell took another shuddering breath. Some colour, not much, came back to his face. Connor noticed that his hands were clenching and unclenching into fists by his side, but he was sure that it was more a sign of distress than of aggression.

Lowell shook his head a little, as if trying to clear it. To convince himself that he wasn't seeing things. 'What are you doing here?' he finally managed to croak.

Oriana swallowed. 'This is home,' she said simply.

'Not any more,' Lowell said harshly.

Oriana flinched. But said nothing. A tiny tic was pulsing at his jaw, and she could see that he had his teeth tightly clenched together. His whole body seemed to be quivering, very finely, like a tautly wired bow after an arrow had been shot. And she wondered, bleakly, when she'd feel the impact of the arrow in her heart. For she had no doubt that she was his target.

It was then that Lowell's eyes flickered, moving a little behind her and to the left. Instinctively, she looked over her shoulder and saw Connor. Big. Alert. Ready. He was standing beside an overgrown mahonia bush and she managed to smile at him. He was glad to see it, but it was a very shaky smile indeed. If the poor bastard opposite her was suffering, then in that moment Connor had no doubts at all that she was matching his suffering, pain for pain. What the hell was going on? What had this pair done to each other?

But, of course, he thought he knew the answer. Or at least had a good idea where it might lie.

'This is Connor O'Dell. Connor, Lowell Seton,' Oriana introduced them shakily.

Lowell stared at Connor blankly. He was aware, dimly, that he didn't like the big man. He didn't like the fact that he knew Oriana, and resented even more the fact that he was here. Now. With her. And he thought he knew why this was so, in some distant part of himself. But he didn't want to explore that avenue. Not now – not ever.

He blinked, trying desperately to rally himself. His brain, always his best ally, seemed to have gone AWOL on him.

'Hello, Lowell,' Connor said calmly.

Lowell nodded tersely, then turned back to Oriana. His eyes pinpointed her, like a lepidopterist with a long steel pin, about to anchor a beautiful butterfly to his specimen table. And she *was* beautiful. Still. Unbelievably beautiful, just as he remembered her.

The same mass of blonde curls. The same lovely eyes. The deceptively fragile-looking figure.

And the face that lied.

It looked like a gentle face. It looked honest. As if the owner of it had laid out all her wares openly, for all to see. Once, Lowell had thought he could see her. But he'd been wrong. Now, looking closely, all he could see was the hardness. It was there, unmistakably, in the wariness which veiled her eyes. He didn't think that Oriana needed that defence. It never once occurred to him that thirteen years in prison was bound to give a person a hard veneer. It certainly never occurred to him that, underneath it all, there might be a woman, broken and in tears, holding herself together by sheer force of will.

'I want you gone,' Lowell said, and knew, even as he said it, that it wasn't entirely true. Oh, it was his first thought, all right. He even believed that 99.9% of himself wanted just that. But it was that other minute sliver, the tiny kernel which was at the very core of him, that rebelled. Given its head, that rotten core inside him would have him drag her into his arms and smother her lovely lying face with kisses.

But Lowell would never set it free. He'd rather die.

As Rollo had died.

Oriana swallowed hard. 'Yes, I daresay you do want me gone,' she said, with infinite, utter sadness. Connor heard it clearly, for it rang like the mythical bell of a church long buried in a massive flood. He'd never before in his life heard anybody sound so utterly hopeless. But he wondered if, in his present state, Lowell Seton was capable of hearing it too. Somehow, he didn't think so.

'But I've been hired to do a job here,' Oriana went on, her voice almost toneless now, 'and I intend to see it through. I'm a qualified interior designer,' her eyes flickered to Connor. 'I took courses for it inside. And the new owners of the Manor have already got architects' plans to convert the place into six flats,' she added, looking back to Lowell. 'Now they want me to come up with plans for the designs. That means living in for a few months,' she finished, waving a hand vaguely at the big, silent house behind her.

It was a lie, of course. All of it. She hadn't done a course in interior design, and had no intention of turning Lowell's home into flats. When this was all over, she intended to turn the house over to him, intact and whole. But she could hardly tell him that now. Not that it would have done much good, for Lowell hardly seemed to hear her.

43

'You're not welcome here,' he said, wondering why he was still standing here, uttering such useless banalities. This was Oriana. The woman who'd destroyed everything. *Everything.* Why did he feel the need to hold her and comfort her? It was insane. Perhaps that was it. Perhaps, in the last few minutes, he'd lost his mind.

'I'm sorry about that,' Oriana said. And meant it. 'But I'm not leaving.'

It was the defiance that did it. Lowell didn't know what to expect from her. Perhaps repentance. Or bravado. Or . . . something. But not defiance. His face tightened ominously, and he took a step towards her. He had no idea what he was going to do, but then, he never got the chance to do it. For suddenly, her lovely, tense, beautiful face was blocked out by the bulk of Connor O'Dell.

He was taller and bigger than Lowell. But Lowell didn't care. He raised his head up; tormented grey eyes met coolly assessing green ones, and Lowell moved. It would take more than this big ape to scare him. At the same time, Connor put out one hand, massive and powerful, and splayed it across his chest.

'Why don't you go home, Mr Seton,' Connor said quietly.

It was the words, the very reasonable words, which cut through his miasma of misery, and cleared his head. Lowell took a step back, staring coldly at Connor's outstretched hand. Without a word, the big man lowered his arm.

Coldness washed over Lowell. His eyes narrowed for a moment on Connor, then he turned and walked away, back to the Dower House, where Margaret Wright was waiting for him impatiently.

Connor watched Lowell Seton until he was out of sight, then slowly relaxed, and turned to Oriana. She looked beaten.

'I take it that he's the man you're afraid of?' Connor said quietly, about to add that, in his judgement, she didn't have much to worry about. A good and instant judge of character, Connor was already sure that Lowell Seton was too much of a man to ever pose a physical threat to a woman. But, again, Oriana surprised him.

'Oh no,' she said softly. 'Lowell isn't the problem. Or at least,' she said, her voice cracking, 'he's my problem. But he's not the danger.'

Connor nodded. So she already knew. He vowed to be much more alert from now on. If Oriana thought that she had another enemy, and a real threat, moreover, one who *was* capable of trying something on, then he was inclined, now more than ever, to believe her. Besides, not many women could go through such an emotional upheaval as she just had, and still think clearly. Whatever problem she had with Lowell Seton, it didn't look easily solvable to him.

'What did you do to him?' he asked, curiously.

Oriana shook her head. 'I didn't do anything to him,' she said softly. 'But he thinks I killed his brother.'

* * *

Lowell pulled his car into the big communal garage, next to the vintage Rolls-Royce, and turned off the engine. He couldn't believe that he'd just taken Margaret to Stratford-upon-Avon as if nothing had happened.

He had vague memories of dancing, of drinking orange juice, of talking to her and taking her home, of kissing her and somehow coming up with some excuse for not staying the night. He had vague memories too of her looking at him with puzzled, resentful eyes. So perhaps he hadn't put on such a good performance after all. Or maybe all this was a dream. He'd wake up in a moment, in his own bed, sweating and maybe even crying.

Oriana would still be in prison. And he'd be . . . Lowell closed his eyes and leaned across the roof of his Daimler, resting his head on his forearms.

He'd be what? Just where he'd always been. With Margaret waiting for him to make the proposal of marriage he could never make. With the prospect of buying back the

Manor still just tantalizingly out of reach. With himself every bit as much in prison as the murderess who'd killed Rollo. Only his prison was of his own making. Damn it, why couldn't he forget her? He'd never even kissed her. Never once told her what he'd felt. Hell, they'd only been sixteen then. How was it that he continued to give her the power to make his life hell?

He opened his eyes to the weary acknowledgement that this was not a dream. He hadn't even the comfort of a nightmare to fall back on. He was standing in his garage, at one o'clock in the morning, and Oriana was living at the Manor. He closed the garage doors and walked, not to the rear entrance, which opened into a small hall and the old servants' staircase leading up to his private suite of rooms. No. There was only one place he could go now.

He walked to the small cottage at the back of the estate.

* * *

Mercedes jumped as she was abruptly catapulted from sleep. For a second she lay there on her mattress, warm and drowsily content, unsure what had woken her. Then she heard it again. The sharp rap of the door knocker.

What on earth? She glanced at the luminous dial of her alarm clock. It read 1.09.

She sat up, reaching for her nightgown and, slipping into it as she padded downstairs, she tried to tell herself that she wasn't frightened. But of course, she was. Nobody came knocking on your door at this time of night with *good* news.

The hall light illuminated a familiar figure beyond the old glass in the door, and she felt herself wilt with relief.

It was Lowell. So at least it wasn't a policeman come to tell her that he'd crashed his car into a tree somewhere. Lowell, she was now very much aware, was all the family she had left.

She opened the door, smiling in relief, and felt the ground underfoot lurch at the look on his face. She stepped back, indicating the kitchen. 'Come inside. I'll put the kettle on,' she said flatly, as if normality could somehow defeat whatever catastrophe had painted that bleak landscape onto her brother's face.

Lowell slumped into the nearest kitchen chair and watched his sister make tea. He wondered, vaguely, why she wasn't married. At twenty-nine she was beautiful, ran her own business, and owned property. He'd thought that her last boyfriend might pop the question, but for some reason he'd faded out.

Mercedes, the tea made, sat at the table, pushed the mug towards him, and took a deep breath. 'OK, big bro,' she said, with forced cheerfulness. 'Let's have it.'

'Oriana's back,' Lowell said.

And Mercedes promptly spilt her tea all over the table. She couldn't help it. Her hands jerked so badly, the mug all but went flying. She got up on shaky legs and went to the sink, returned with a dish cloth, and wiped up the mess. She was literally incapable of speech.

'She's staying at the Manor, of all places,' Lowell went on. 'Apparently, the new owners have hired her to do some work there.' He was surprised how her every word was ingrained on his memory. At the time, it had all seemed to happen in a fog.

Mercedes sat back down and managed to take a swallow of her depleted tea. It went down like acid. So Oriana was back. And Mercedes could no longer pretend she didn't exist. As she had been pretending for the last thirteen years.

Grimly, she let the barriers down.

Oriana Foster had been Mercedes' best friend since forever. They were the same age, had grown up in the same village, and had gone to the same schools. Little wonder, then, that they should have been friends. But it had been more than that. They'd been like sisters. Even the schoolteachers referred to them as that. The sisters. It was semi-ironic. With Oriana so curly-haired and fair, and Mercedes with her straight, long, raven hair, they couldn't have looked more different. And yet they thought the same. Wanted the same things. Talked a secret language. And, unlike most children, shared everything together. Toys. Make-up. Comics. Sweets. You name it, Mercedes and Oriana were willing to go halves.

As primary-school kids, it had been understandable. But, with puberty, there had been none of the usual petty squabbles which went with intense friendship. Their friendship had even survived the battering of moving on to the big local comprehensive. Not even that huge, sprawling school had been able to sweep them up and toss them apart, as it had so many other firm chums.

Instead, their friendship had matured. When Oriana's parents had been killed in the car crash when Oriana was just fifteen, it had been Mercedes, more than her aunt, whom Oriana had gone to for comfort. Oh, her mother's much older sister, also a resident of Nether Dene, had taken her in most willingly, but had had no idea how to comfort her.

But Mercedes had.

It had seemed the two girls were destined to be lifelong friends. Bridesmaids at each other's weddings. Godparents to each other's children. And when Rollo had taken such a liking to her, and they had started going out, Mercedes had been over the moon, imagining Oriana as her sister-in-law. An official sister to her at last. But then it had all fallen apart. One night, over thirteen years ago, the dream had ended. And not only ended, but transmogrified into a nightmare which just went on and on and on.

Mercedes had fallen apart after her best friend had been convicted of murdering her older brother. She'd coped only by pretending that Oriana had never existed. Whenever she found herself remembering some incident that involved her old friend, she simply cut it off and thought of something else.

But now, with Lowell's terse, flat words, she knew she'd have to change her whole strategy for survival. And had no idea what that might be. For some reason, the big blond man she'd met yesterday came flashing into her mind.

48

'*But why did she come back?*' Mercedes wailed suddenly. 'Why come here? *Here* of all places? It's so cruel. It's so unlike her.'

And then she put a hand to her mouth, appalled. She sounded like a hysterical harpy. And what she'd said was so stupid. For Oriana was a murderess. Why should cruelty be beyond her? When would she learn that her wonderful friend of childhood no longer existed? And why, after all this time, should it still hurt so?

Lowell shook his head grimly. 'I don't know why she came back. But I can tell you this. She won't stay. Not if I have anything to do with it.'

* * *

The next morning, Lowell wrote the letter. It had taken him a few phone calls, and he'd called in a few favours, but he'd got the name and address of the company who'd bought his old home. Uninspiringly called OxonCountryProp Developments, it had offices in Headington.

The letter was clear and reasonable. It pointed out that Oriana Foster was not the ideal employee, since she had a record for murder, and that the villagers of Nether Dene, and himself and his sister in particular, objected to Oriana Foster's presence there. It was clever and hard-hitting. As he posted it, Lowell had no doubts at all that OxonCountryProp, anxious to sell their newly converted flats, would be only too willing to avoid any adverse publicity or local backlash (a threat which could be read between every line of the letter), and dismiss Ms Foster on the spot.

Later, Lowell intended to follow up with an offer to buy the property. But, in order for them to bite, he knew he would have to make it a good one. He knew he might have to sell the hotel.

He was just walking back from the post box when he saw Miss Craddock. Miss Craddock, now well into her seventies, had been a teacher at the village primary school all her working life. She'd taught not only himself, Mercedes and Rollo, but their father's generation as well. She was instantly recognizable as what she was, with her grey hair pinned back in a chignon, comfortable black lace-up shoes, and a smart tweed suit, a copy of which she ordered from Scotland every ten years or so.

'Hello, Miss Craddock. Need a lift to Banbury?' he asked.

Since the village shop had closed down, he knew most of the village's older residents usually went into the nearby market town on a Thursday.

He wasn't heading that way himself, but he wouldn't mind taking her.

Miss Craddock turned her bespectacled face to him and smiled warmly. 'Thank you, Lowell, but I've not long returned from Bicester.' The voice was exactly as he remembered it from the school room – crisply enunciated, perfectly proper, Queen's English. Lowell, like everyone else in the village, had the utmost respect for Miss Craddock. She might never have married, or, so one would think, sampled life at all, but she was the best judge of character bar none. She stood for no nonsense. Firmly knew right from wrong, and, along with the vicar, was the one person you went to when in need. She was, in fact, just the sort of ally Lowell needed if he was to succeed in making Oriana leave the village.

'Miss Craddock, did you know that Oriana Foster is back here? In Nether Dene?' he asked softly.

Miss Craddock stiffened. It was one of the few times that he'd ever seen her disconcerted. 'No. Indeed I did not. I'm pleased to hear it.'

Lowell was sure he'd misheard her. He looked at her uncertainly, and, once again, had the rare but rather frightening experience of seeing her disconcerted.

'I'm sorry, Lowell. That was very tactless of me,' she said, sincerely. But she didn't, he noticed, take it back.

'I'm not sure I understand,' he said. 'Why should you be pleased that she's back? Surely you don't think it a good idea that she lives here. Even for a short while.'

50

Miss Craddock did, in fact, believe just that, but she could hardly say so to Lowell. For Miss Craddock had never believed Oriana Foster to be guilty of the murder of Rollo Seton. She'd attended every day of the trial, and listened very carefully to all the evidence, which was utterly damning; but she'd also listened to Oriana's testimony. It had been, on the whole, a rather pathetic performance, for what could the poor girl say, except that she hadn't done it? That she hadn't been there. The jury had not believed her. But then, the jury hadn't taught her for over seven years. The jury didn't have Miss Craddock's vast knowledge of children, and the people they grew up to be. But the schoolteacher had been lied to by all sorts over the years. She knew when it was happening, and when it wasn't.

So Miss Craddock knew, in her heart of hearts, that Oriana Foster's story was true. And, because of this, she believed that a grave miscarriage of justice had been done on the day that Oriana had been sentenced for the murder of Rollo Seton. But, of course, she could say none of this to his brother, Lowell. It just wasn't done. He, after all, was one of the many victims of that dark deed, and Miss Craddock had no desire to add to his burden.

But she had no desire to give him a false impression either. Something of her thoughts must have shown in her face, for Lowell stared at her, totally aghast.

'Miss Craddock, surely you of all people can understand how Mercedes and I feel about this?'

Miss Craddock's face softened. 'Yes. I understand that perfectly. But, Lowell,' she said, and laid her bony, rather arthritic hand on his arm, 'Oriana maintained, and has always maintained, her innocence.'

Lowell shook her hand off, and, not trusting himself to speak, turned and walked away. What the hell was happening to his world? What was wrong with people? That Miss Craddock, *Miss Craddock* of all people, should have been taken in by Oriana Foster. As he got into his car and drove away, he wondered if anybody else in the village thought the same way as she did. But he knew that they didn't. They couldn't. But, he suddenly wondered, would they have been likely to tell him if they had? Nobody ever talked to him about Rollo. Not even Mercedes.

The incident with Miss Craddock had shaken him almost as much as his first sight of Oriana herself. For the first time in his life, Lowell felt like going home and getting drunk. So drunk that he'd never even have to wake up tomorrow.

* * *

Connor was watching out for her this time, and sure enough, come mid-morning, here she was. He went out the back door swiftly, cut across the rear of the gardens, and emerged onto the overgrown footpath.

Mercedes looked up and smiled. Somehow, she wasn't surprised to see him.

'Hello, isn't it lovely out?' she asked cheerfully. He looked even more attractive than she remembered, and today was dressed in dark green slacks and a grey pullover.

He grinned and pushed his floppy dark blond hair off his forehead with an impatient hand. 'It's great out. I was just thinking of going for a hike myself.'

'Good idea,' she grinned back at him. That morning, Mercedes had gone into the hotel and, under cover of chatting to the receptionist, had scanned the register. There were plenty of couples registered, but only two single male names which she'd been able to see. Otto Schoenhoven, and Riley Caine.

And he certainly didn't look or speak like an Otto!

She wondered what he'd do if she cheekily greeted him by name, but decided against it. Some men didn't like being checked up on.

Connor smiled. 'I was hoping you'd let me walk with you. Seeing as I don't know the area.'

Mercedes eyes twinkled. 'I'd love to. Unfortunately, I'm just on my way back. But if you like, I can pick you up at the hotel tomorrow, and we can go for a six-mile jaunt.'

Connor groaned. 'You do know how to tempt a man, don't you? But if I walk you home now, and find out where you live, I can come and collect you. Now that's a far more gentlemanly arrangement.'

Mercedes laughed, enjoying the game. The first few tentative steps of courtship always seemed, in some way, to be the sweetest. 'So it is. I might even be persuaded to give you some breakfast. Dry toast and prunes.'

'Oh, be still my heart,' he sighed, theatrically clutching his massive hands to his equally massive chest.

'Don't push your luck!' Mercedes gurgled, wondering what he'd look like minus that sweater. Magnificent. That's what.

They moved through the overgrown laurels, stepping out on to the road just past the church. To Connor's surprise, however, instead of turning left, into the village square, which led on to the village proper, she turned right. Surely that was a dead end down there? Weren't the vicarage and the Dower House Hotel the only buildings down there? She wasn't the parson's daughter, surely? He groaned to himself, wondering how he'd ever persuade a mild but knowing country vicar that he was a suitable partner for his daughter. A rough-and-ready ex-soldier, with little family and no academic qualifications to recommend him, was hardly likely to impress Papa.

For Connor was beginning to feel this might hold some promise. There was something about this beautiful, dark-haired temptress which was making him feel hopeful for the future. Something in the way she slipped her hand into his, without coyness, as if it belonged there. Which it did.

But Mercedes led him past the big, rather ugly facade of the vicarage, and on to a small picket fence. Beyond it, he saw with delighted surprise, was a small stone cottage, simple and exquisitely proportioned, set in the most ravishing garden he'd seen in a long time.

'This is my place,' Mercedes said simply, but she'd seen the look in his eyes and was glad. People, when presented with her cottage and traditional garden, either loved it or hated it. She was glad that Riley loved it. So glad. She couldn't imagine living anywhere else.

'Columbines,' he said happily, pointing out the intricately shaped flowers growing next to the fence. 'My granny loved columbines.'

'Your granny had good taste.'

Connor glanced uncertainly to the right, and the big edifice of the hotel. 'Isn't it noisy though? Living right next to that place?'

'Not at all. Besides, Lowell wouldn't have given me the cottage if he hadn't known how much I loved it.'

Connor stiffened and stared at her. 'Lowell? You mean Lowell Seton?' What was he doing *giving* her cottages? A shaft of jealousy turned Connor's green eyes even greener.

Mercedes laughed. 'Who else? He's my brother,' she said. And then, realizing that they'd never been formally introduced, held out her hand. 'I'm Mercedes Seton.'

But even as Connor automatically took her fingers in his, his big hands engulfing her own, thrilling her with their sense of restrained, gentle power, she felt something go wrong. Something change.

'I'm Connor O'Dell,' Connor said gruffly.

'Oh,' she said. So she'd got his name wrong. But that, she felt sure, was not all she'd got wrong. Something had happened to his eyes. Mercedes could almost feel the shutters come down and wanted to cry out in protest. Why? What was wrong? It was all going so well. Wasn't it? Surely she couldn't have misread the signs.

Connor smiled stiffly. 'Nice to meet you, Mercedes Seton,' he said.

But he didn't mean it.

Why couldn't she have been Mercedes Smith, or Mercedes Jones? Mercedes anyone else other than Seton. Because he might easily have become the lover of Mercedes Smith. Wouldn't have minded being the long-term boyfriend of Mercedes Jones. Would happily have asked out Mercedes anyone else, and seen where it took them.

But what could he possibly do with Mercedes Seton, except keep his distance?

FIVE

Connor smiled uncomfortably. 'Well, I have to be off. I'll be seeing you sometime,' he said, cringing inside, even as he heard himself speak. If he sounded false and standoffish to his own ears, what must she be thinking?

Mercedes watched him backing off, wondering what had happened to their breakfast date tomorrow. Somehow, she didn't think he'd be keeping it. 'Connor,' she said quickly, her eyes darkening, as he turned blank eyes back on to her. What had happened to all that twinkle? All that *knowledge*? That age-old, intuitive, male-female seesaw knowhow which didn't need words. Why, in fact, was he suddenly a complete stranger again?

Mercedes shook her head, as she realized he was still waiting for her to speak. 'Nothing,' she said numbly. 'Have a good time. Wherever it is you're going.' Now why had she said that? It sounded pathetic. The last thing she wanted was to give him the impression she was needy. Because she wasn't.

Connor sighed heavily. She didn't want him to go. He didn't want to go. By rights, they should be sitting in that lovely little cottage of hers by now, drinking tea, and maybe even touching a little.

56

He turned and went away. As he walked up the road, careful not to turn into the main gates of the Manor, just in case she was still watching him, Connor gave himself a good mental kicking. But what else could he have done? As he went in the side entrance to the ramshackle big house, his mind went back to the first day he'd met Oriana. He'd asked her what she'd been in prison for, and she'd told him it was murder. No messing about, no prevarication, no self-justification. Just a simple statement. Then she'd waited a moment or two, to give him time to digest the information, and then had asked him quietly if it made any difference to his taking the job. Why hadn't he said that, yes, it did? Normally he would have done, and promptly terminated the interview. So why hadn't he? Instinct. That was all. And perhaps curiosity. Maybe he'd become a little bored, and sensed, in the quiet, beautiful, self-contained blonde woman, that here was a case way beyond the usual run of the mill. Connor was a big boy, and he'd played some hard games in the past, especially in the Gulf. He could take care of himself, and that included taking responsibility for his actions.

And the truth was, before he'd found out the identity of his raven-haired, beautiful stranger, he'd no regrets about taking on Oriana's case. He shook his head. Well, he wasn't about to turn his back on Ms Foster now. Having his romantic hopes dashed wasn't, in his opinion, a good enough excuse for backing out on a client.

He wondered, though, for the first time, if Oriana really *had* murdered someone. And not just someone, but Mercedes' brother. At the time, he'd taken it for granted that she had, but probably not in cold blood. After getting to know her, however, he'd begun to wonder if she'd been capable even of manslaughter. Then, after her run-in with Lowell Seton, he'd been all but convinced of her innocence. Now, because of his attraction for Mercedes, the sister of the victim, he was back to wondering again. Not that it would matter to him, one way or the other. Oriana was his client, and needed protection. She was paying him, and he'd protect her. Simple.

And it was not as if his feelings for Mercedes could ever come to anything. Not now. For once she found out that he was (supposedly) Oriana's boyfriend, she'd probably start to hate his guts. And who could blame her?

Hell, what a mess!

* * *

Two days later, Connor watched uneasily as Oriana slowly lowered a bouquet of sweet williams on to the humped earth. They were in the churchyard, and she'd just finished tending to the graves of what were obviously her parents and, he guessed, an aunt. He'd wondered who the last of the flowers were for, and now he could see for himself.

The grave belonged to Rollo Seton.

Connor couldn't help but watch her face closely as she looked at the headstone of the man everyone believed she had murdered. Surely no murderess would have the gall to take flowers to a victim's grave. Would she? It would take a woman without a heart to do that, and Connor was sure that Oriana had a heart all right. And one, moreover, which was breaking.

Oriana looked down at the lichen-covered stone, at the words inscribed on it, and into her mind came memories of the man. Rollo Seton, aged nineteen. A little big-headed (he was, after all, the son of the Lord of the Manor). Good-looking, fun-loving. A little greedy. But basically a normal human being.

He hadn't deserved to be killed.

She slowly reached into the pocket of her jeans and drew out the small heart-shaped locket which she had last looked at on the day she had got out of prison. It was a cheap little thing – gold plated – the chain not even that. A tiny rhinestone sparkled in the centre. Oriana smiled tenderly. Rollo, always careful with money. And why not? They'd only been going out a month or so, but it had been her sixteenth birthday. It was, she supposed, a natural enough compromise – a piece of jewellery, but nothing expensive.

Connor, catching the small, sad smile, turned and walked slowly over to the long, low wall which surrounded the churchyard, and leaned against it, to give her some privacy.

* * *

Further down the lane, Lowell, Mercedes and Margaret Wright came out of the Dower House Hotel and walked to where Margaret had parked her BMW convertible. In the back, she had stowed all her archery gear. A gifted amateur, she was on her way to a local competition, and Lowell and Mercedes were her cheering party. They chatted and laughed as they neared the churchyard gates, but Oriana, lost in thought, didn't hear them. She was thinking instead about how unfair life could be. To her. To Rollo. To everyone.

As she gazed at the stone and his name, she wondered what kind of man he'd be now, had he lived. He certainly would have been married, but not to her. Theirs had been a tenuous romance at best, and would almost certainly have fizzled out rapidly, if only because Rollo would have wanted their relationship to progress to a more physical level. And Oriana wouldn't have allowed that.

She looked back to the naive teenager she'd been, with all her hopes and dreams, and shook her head at her folly. It was amazing what time did to you.

Rollo, for instance, would have matured, would have lost some of his youthful smugness, would have finished university, got a job, mellowed, married, been a father himself by now. He'd have developed a much more three-dimensional character than he'd had back then. Adolescence would, for him, be a thing of the past, as it was for her now. It seemed so unfair that he should be cut down before he'd had the chance to mature.

Oriana sighed heavily and rubbed her eyes. She hoped Rollo had never guessed the truth about things. The truth about herself. Of what she'd done to him. For it had definitely been unfair. If she hadn't been so young herself, so unsure, so desperately in love, she'd never have even contemplated treating him so shabbily. No, she hoped he'd never guessed. And she didn't really think he had. He'd been too sure of himself to ever suspect . . .

'What the devil do you think you're doing?'

Oriana jumped and spun around. A giddying sense of déjà vu hit her as she was once more face to face with Lowell. A white-faced, furious Lowell. He was dressed in grey slacks and a black-and-white geometric shirt. With his raven hair, square face and blazing eyes he was heart-stoppingly good-looking.

By the wall, Connor straightened up and began to walk towards them.

Oriana's eyes flickered as, either side of Lowell, first Mercedes then Margaret appeared.

Margaret was dressed in tight-fitting black slacks and a military-style matching tunic top with flat brass buttons. Her hair was held back by a floating, black chiffon scarf. Her make-up was flawless. Real pearls glistened in her small ears. Her small, dark-brown eyes bored into Oriana with a mixture of curiosity and venom.

Oriana didn't look at her long. She couldn't. Her eyes moved instead to Mercedes. Her old friend looked good, but she, too, was pale. She wondered if she was married. If she had children yet.

'Hello, Mercy,' she said softly.

Mercedes blinked. 'Hello, Orrie,' she said stiffly. Mercedes felt distinctly odd. She'd thought that this moment would be torture. After Lowell had woken her in the early hours to tell her of Oriana's return, she'd lain awake all the rest of that night, imagining this very meeting. Dreading it. Rehearsing things she might say. Trying to come up with hurtful, dignified, cutting sentences. But now that she was face to face with Oriana, Mercedes didn't want to hurt her. She wanted to ask her: why?

Why? Why? Why?

'I asked you a question,' Lowell said, bringing Oriana's eyes rocketing back to his.

She was wearing a pale gold summer dress and white sandals. She looked young and fresh and lovely, like a buttercup. Still the woman of his dreams. His nightmares. Lowell dragged his eyes from her, and down on to his brother's grave, and the multi-coloured flowers lying there, like an accusation.

'Did you put those there?' he snapped.

Connor came closer. As he did so, he saw Mercedes' head lift, as if sensing danger, and over the headstones, their eyes met. Her face lit up. She began to smile. Connor didn't smile back. Instead he came on, slowly, carefully, watchfully.

'Yes, I brought them,' Oriana said simply, and Margaret Wright caught her breath. 'Well, you have to admire the woman's gall, Lowell,' she said harshly.

'I don't have to do any such thing,' Lowell snarled. 'Take them off. Now!'

Oriana didn't move. She met his gaze unflinchingly. 'Why should I do that, Lowell?' she asked softly.

Lowell stiffened, pain and incredulity washing over his face, and Oriana had to fight the desire to go to him and hold his face in her hands, to whisper to him words which would take away once and for all the pain and hurt and confusion which were obviously tormenting him. But of course, she couldn't.

'You can ask me that?' he finally said. 'You killed him, and you dare bring him flowers?'

Oriana shook her head. 'I dare bring him flowers because I didn't kill him,' she said flatly. Her words weren't loud, but they carried across the churchyard clearly.

Mercedes gasped. 'You're *still* saying that?' she asked, stunned. She knew that Oriana had pleaded not guilty of course, although she hadn't felt able to attend many days of the trial. But since her conviction, it had never occurred to her that her old friend would go on denying her guilt.

Oriana turned and looked at Mercedes. 'Yes, I'm still saying it, because it's still true. I wasn't at the house that night. I didn't argue with Rollo. I didn't say I wanted to kill him, and I certainly didn't push him down the stairs, deliberately or otherwise.'

Connor was now almost level with them, but he halted just behind Oriana. His gut instinct had told him she wasn't a murderer, but this was the first time she'd come out and flatly denied it. It made him feel better about things. A lot better.

Even so, the puzzled look Mercedes was giving him now had his muscles tightening in protest, and his heart already beginning to fortify itself against some nasty moments he knew must be about to come. Strange how a woman he'd barely met could tie him up in knots so quickly.

'That's not what the housekeeper said,' Margaret drawled, her upper-crust voice cutting across the atmosphere and turning it, once again, poisonous.

Oriana looked at Margaret and said nothing.

Lowell smiled crookedly. 'Nothing to say?' he jeered.

Oriana shook her head. What could she say? That she was looking into it – or rather, that she had a team of private detectives looking into it? No – they would want to know how she had the money for such an expensive undertaking, and she could not tell them about the fortune sitting in her bank. If her theory was correct – and she didn't see how it could be wrong – to talk about it would expose another person to danger. She was willing to take all kinds of risks with her own life to find out the truth and clear her name, but she wasn't about to take chances with somebody else's.

Even if it meant taking every sling and arrow thrown at her.

Besides, at that moment, she literally had no proof that the Setons' housekeeper had lied, so what could she have said anyway?

Lowell reached down and removed the flowers. Their sweet scent made him feel slightly sick. He tossed them aside contemptuously, and Oriana paled even further. She made no move to retrieve them, however.

'I never intended to offend you, Lowell,' she said, her eyes then flickering to his sister. 'Or you, Mercy. I'll go.'

'What a good idea,' Margaret said sardonically. Her eyes, however, were on Connor. A big, good-looking man, but who the hell was he? And what was he doing butting in on a private conversation?

Oriana turned away, saw Connor and reached out her hand. It was both a public display – to implant in everyone's mind Connor's cover as her boyfriend – but he could see it was more than that. Much more. She needed a friendly face. A helping hand. He reached out, squeezing her fingers in a silent message of support. Chin up, girl.

Mercedes' jaw dropped. She shot Connor an amazed look, but he wasn't watching her. He was watching Oriana instead. And his expression puzzled her. For all that Oriana had turned to him, and he'd taken her hand in his, he didn't look at her as a lover might. There was concern, but not enough concern. He didn't look outraged, or embarrassed but loyal, or grim, or any of the things which Mercedes was sure a real boyfriend *would* feel, after having witnessed such a scene. Instead he looked . . . She battled to find the right words, but couldn't. He looked many things. Calm. Controlled. Alert. Patient. Had she but known it, the word she sought so desperately was 'professional'. Or perhaps she was just seeing what she wanted to see. That she didn't want to admit to herself that she'd made a mistake about her craggy-faced blond giant.

'Are you all right?' Connor asked Oriana quietly.

Oriana nodded, but her knees felt weak and shaky. And it wasn't only what Lowell had done which had made her feel so shattered, either: it was meeting Margaret Wright for the first time.

Lowell's eyes darkened hopelessly as he watched Oriana turn to Connor O'Dell. It made him ache, in every atom, to see the big man touch her. To take her hand and steer her gently away from harm.

Harm called Lowell Seton.

He wanted to yell out at her to leave him alone. To come to him, Lowell, for comfort. To rely on *his* strength, to cry on *his* shoulder, to let him take care of her. But what kind of madness was that?

'Come on, Lowell, let's go,' Margaret said, reaching out and firmly pushing her hand through the crook of his arm. He felt as taut as a bowstring, and she didn't like the way he was staring after Oriana Foster. Of course, it was to be expected that he'd react strongly to her presence, but there was something about the intensity of his eyes when he looked at her that Margaret didn't like. Didn't like one little bit.

But maybe she was imagining it. After all, Oriana had only just turned sixteen at the time of Rollo's murder, as had Lowell himself. And Oriana had been *Rollo's* girlfriend, not Lowell's. There could have been nothing between Lowell and Oriana then. And for the last thirteen years, the girl had been in prison. No, when she thought she sensed a connection between them, she must have been imagining things. Still, it wouldn't hurt to remind him who belonged to whom.

'Come on. After I've won the cup you can take me somewhere nice and quiet to celebrate,' she whispered huskily in his ear, and stood on tiptoe to kiss his neck.

Lowell, still staring after Oriana, barely felt it.

Mercedes, too, was watching Oriana and Connor as they walked away, but her eyes were more puzzled.

So he wasn't a guest at the Dower House. Looking back, she could see now how cleverly he'd avoided admitting as much. And something else made sense too, now: the way he'd shut down the other day. Things had been going well until they'd arrived at her house, and Connor had learned that she was Mercedes Seton. It had been that which had brought the shutters down and turned off the light of sexual awareness and interest in his lovely green eyes. But it didn't make sense.

If Connor was Oriana's boyfriend, then Connor must be the two-timing type. And that alone didn't seem right. And yet, Mercedes thought ruefully, she was prepared to accept that her instincts in that department might be faulty. What woman could really, honestly say that she could be a hundred per cent sure of herself, and her instincts, when it came to an attractive man? So, say he was the cheating kind. He was with Oriana. He meets and fancies her, Mercedes. It's all systems go. Until he finds out who she is. Then it comes to a screeching stop. Why? If he was the cheating kind, would he really care if she and Oriana shared a past?

And she was still puzzled by his reaction just now. OK, so he'd come over when he could see things were getting heated. He'd stood by her, took her hand, led her away. But he hadn't said anything. Hadn't interfered. Hadn't stuck his own oar in. How many men seeing their girlfriend being badgered by a crowd would stand by so quietly? Like . . . well . . . like an outsider, watching, listening, but not really a part of it all. That still didn't make sense to her. It didn't fit in with Connor's character, which she was sure she could intuit. There was something not quite right here, and . . .

'Come on, Mercedes, we'll be late.' Margaret's impatient, rather nasal voice cut across her reverie and she turned and trudged away. She wished now that she hadn't agreed to go and cheer on Margaret at her archery shoot. She was bound to win anyway. She always did. Mercedes could have done with some quiet time on her own — she had a lot to think about. Instead, she clambered into the back of Margaret's car, and stared unseeingly out of the window. In the front passenger seat, her brother did the same.

* * *

'Thanks for not interfering back there,' Oriana said. They were nearing the Manor now, and the sight of it depressed her. She really would have to get some people in to give it the care and attention it needed.

'That's all right,' Connor said. 'I could see you were handling it.' Besides, he thought silently, it had been none of his business. In his mind's eye, though, he could still see

Mercedes' face as she looked at him. Hurt. Bewildered. But not yet angry. But that would come, and he wondered who he was trying to kid. For he had the nasty feeling that Oriana's business would become his own, and not before much longer.

The mail had arrived, and Oriana leafed through it, stopping when she recognized one, which could only have come from her front man in Headington. Marcus Royle ran a one-man accountancy and business advice service, and he wasn't supposed to write to her here unless it was absolutely necessary. She thought she'd made that clear to him. With a small sigh, she took the letter through to the rather dingy den, glad to have something to take her mind off what had just happened.

Would Lowell ever look at her with anything other than hate? Would she ever glance up and see in his grey eyes the kind of look which he'd given her when they were sixteen, and he'd thought nobody else was watching him? She felt a dry sob catch in her throat, and quickly coughed. Enough of that. It was gone. Over with. Killed, as surely as Rollo had been killed.

She ripped open the envelope and took out two pieces of paper. One, a covering letter from Marcus, briefly explained the enclosed letter, and asked her how she wanted it handled. Oriana quickly cast her eye down to the signature at the bottom and her hand started to shake.

It was from Lowell.

As she read it, she felt the tears roll down her face. Was he so desperate to have her gone that he'd resort to this? The missive was obviously an attempt on his part to get her sacked by her so-called employers, OxonCountryProp Developments. She read it to the very bitter end, and stared down at his signature, which blurred and wavered as the tears came and went, and came again.

In the kitchen, Connor could hear her weeping. He half rose from his chair, then subsided again. Let her cry. He guessed she hadn't cried in years. Besides, what could he do for her? He couldn't help. Only one man, he suspected, could do that. And Lowell Seton, he imagined, would rather die himself before helping Oriana Foster.

Oriana, her fit of weeping over, lay back against the hard, rather uncomfortable leather sofa and rubbed her wet face wearily. She'd have to write back to Marcus and tell him to stall. But she felt too weary to do it now. Too heartsick. Her mind, given the catharsis of tears, found itself going back over the years.

She was sixteen and so utterly in love – with Lowell Seton.

But it had been Rollo who'd asked her out. Rollo, nowhere near as good-looking, but older, more confident. Rollo, who wasn't about to take no for an answer. But why say no, when saying yes meant that she had access to Lowell in a way she never had as Mercy's best friend? Saying 'yes' meant that she got to join Rollo when he and Lowell went fishing. She got to go to the local football games, ostensibly to cheer on Rollo, in reality to watch Lowell, who was much the better player. And Lowell seemed to take every opportunity to be with her too. Or had she only imagined that? On the sofa, thirteen years older and so many more years wiser, Oriana frowned. Had she kidded herself, all those years ago, that Lowell Seton had loved her, even if tentatively? Had he not, after all, talked to her with those soft grey eyes of his, giving her silent messages of encouragement?

But, in the hard, gritty context of the here and now, what did it matter if Lowell really *had* felt puppy love for her? Just because Oriana had spent the last thirteen years locked away, and had never met anyone else or lost her first, powerful love for Lowell Seton, did she really think the same could be said of him? When he and Margaret Wright were obviously lovers? And how many more had there been?

She got up and, as she did so, met her reflection in the mirror as she passed it. She looked like a wan, woebegone ghost. She stared at the hurting, pretty young girl in the glass.

'Get a grip, for pity's sake,' she snarled savagely at her.

* * *

Mercedes wasn't surprised to see him. In fact, she'd been waiting for him, on some subconscious level.

The boxers lounged at her feet, watching with interest the moorhens and mallards on the River Cherwell, whilst, down the towpath, Connor came walking towards her. Margaret's competition was over (she'd taken silver, much to her chagrin), and the sun was setting on another glorious spring evening. When he drew level with her, as she sat on the grass in the shade of a weeping willow, he lowered himself to the ground next to her without a word. It was as if they'd both taken for granted that this moment would happen.

Mercedes took a second or two to admire the way he could manoeuvre his large frame with such grace and economical ease, then smiled grimly.

'So, are you Oriana's boyfriend?' she asked straight away. No hellos. No 'you cheating bastard'. Just a demand for the truth, and the need to hear it.

Connor, unable to give it to her, sighed. 'Do you think so?'

Mercedes shrugged. As an attempt at nonchalance, it was a pathetic failure. 'It's all over the village that you are,' she said.

Connor's lips twisted. 'And the village is always right, is it?'

'No,' Mercedes said sharply. Gossip, in her opinion, often got it wrong. Besides, Lowell had told her about his extraordinary run-in with Miss Craddock and, like him, she'd been wondering just how many other people in Nether Dene shared her view. So she was in no mood to take the opinions of the village as her measuring stick.

'Well then,' Connor said flatly.

'That's no answer,' she snapped. 'And besides, you held her hand.'

'Do I have to be her boyfriend to offer her support in what was clearly a difficult situation?' he said, although not harshly.

Mercedes just sighed.

'I want you to go and speak to Oriana,' Connor said, abruptly changing the subject. He looked at her closely, as if reading some invisible print on her face. 'I think you need to get things sorted out once and for all.'

'What do you mean? Why should I see Oriana, after what she's done?' Mercedes spluttered.

'And what has she done?'

Mercedes flushed. 'You know damned well what. She killed my brother.'

'But what if she didn't?'

And with those simple words, he utterly undermined her. She stared at him, words buzzing around in her head, but failing to fit into any pattern. She wanted him to admit that it was her he wanted, and not Oriana. That it was she, Mercedes, who was important to him. That they were right together. That they couldn't be together, talk together like this, unless it meant something.

To her horror, she felt great big fat tears come to her eyes and she shot up. For a moment she stared down at him, wild-eyed, confused, hurt. Then she ran off so abruptly that even the boxers were taken by surprise. Connor watched them galloping after her, barking in surprise, and shook his head.

Ah, Mercedes. Forgive me. He didn't like to keep her in the dark about his relationship with Oriana. And he felt like all kinds of a heel, making her face up to things which she'd rather keep safely buried. But he wasn't going to give up on her. Not while he was still in with a chance.

SIX

Mercedes felt her hand tremble as she lifted the knocker and rapped twice. What was she doing here? She hoped it would be Connor who answered the door, but when she heard the handle turn a moment later, it was Oriana staring back at her. She looked as shocked to find Mercedes on her doorstep as Mercedes felt to be there.

'Hello,' Oriana said blankly.

'Hello,' Mercedes echoed, somewhat feebly.

Oriana held open the door and stood to one side. 'Come on in. I was just baking something in the kitchen. I'm not sure it's going to come out right, though.'

Mercedes followed Oriana into the kitchen, feeling distinctly weird. She hadn't set foot in the old family home for many years, ever since the crippling inheritance tax they'd had to pay had forced them to sell up. Now everything looked both familiar and different. Oriana put the kettle on as Mercedes sat down awkwardly at the old, battered wooden table. She waited until Oriana, bringing the tea, was settled opposite her, before taking a deep breath.

'I have to tell you, I'm only here because Connor asked me to come,' she said at once.

Oriana looked at her with such obvious surprise that Mercedes knew Connor couldn't have told her about their conversation last evening, which pleased her enormously.

'Oh?' Oriana said. She didn't ask how Mercedes had come to know her boyfriend, which Mercedes found odd. Nor did she ask why Mercedes felt compelled to do as he asked, which she found even more odd.

'He said I should hear you out,' Mercedes said flatly.

Oriana gave a wry smile. 'That was nice of him. But unless you have an open mind on the subject, I don't think there'd be much point.'

Mercedes blinked. She hadn't expected Oriana to be so matter-of-fact. So unemotional about everything. It put Mercedes on the defensive, for some reason.

'Look, why don't you just say what you have to say, and I'll listen, and we'll take it from there?' she said, her voice hard-edged with just a tinge of anger.

Oriana looked at her and nodded. 'All right. But before I begin, let me ask you a question. Supposing you and Lowell and everybody else were right, and I really did kill Rollo. Why have I come back?'

Mercedes swallowed hard. Wasn't that just the question she'd been asking herself, ever since she'd learned of Oriana's return?

'I don't know,' she said flatly.

'It doesn't make sense, does it? There's nothing for me here now – even my aunt's dead. And I certainly have no friends here.' She grimaced. 'It would make sense for me to have started a new life in London, or gone anywhere else but here, where people know me, and point at me in the street.'

Mercedes nodded, willing to acknowledge that it couldn't be pleasant for Oriana to live here. So why was she putting herself in such an uncomfortable situation when she didn't need to? 'OK. So tell me. Why are you here?' she challenged.

Oriana raised her mug of tea to her lips, took a sip, her blue eyes fixed on Mercedes' own anxious hazel gaze.

'Because, Mercedes, if I didn't kill Rollo, it means someone else did,' she said calmly.

Mercedes reached blindly for her own mug, its warmth feeling extra hot against the coldness of her fingers. She managed to swallow piping-hot tea, and the buzzing in her head slowly faded.

Oriana smiled. 'You see, I have a distinct advantage over everyone else: I *know* I didn't do it.'

At the trial, the pathologist told how he'd found bruising, similar to the flat heel of a human palm, in the middle of Rollo's chest, indicating that someone had most definitely given him a ferocious push. There could be no question of an accidental fall.

'So, I asked myself,' Oriana continued gently, 'where am I going to find the answers which prove my innocence? Where am I going to find Rollo's real killer?' Oriana shrugged helplessly. 'Here, where else? Unless we're to accept the premise that Rollo was killed by a total stranger, a passing maniac who had nothing to do with Nether Dene. And I simply don't buy that.'

Mercedes slowly put down her mug. 'It all sounds very reasonable, but you're forgetting Mrs Greer's testimony,' she pointed out coldly.

Frances Greer had been her family's housekeeper for over two years when Rollo died. Mercedes had never particularly liked her, and neither had Lowell, since she was a tyrant in the kitchen and was forever complaining about the mess they caused, but she had no reason, as far as Mercedes could tell, to lie. And she had told the court that, on the afternoon of Rollo's death, she'd heard Oriana and Rollo arguing. What's more, that she'd distinctly heard Oriana scream, 'I'm going to kill you!' or something very similar, just before she heard the sound of Rollo's body careering down the stairs.

Oriana smiled grimly. 'Oh no,' she said. 'I'm not forgetting Mrs Greer.'

'I don't understand,' Mercedes said. And she didn't. Yet she was beginning to hope, stupidly, naively, that Oriana was telling the truth. How wonderful it would be if it was true! She'd have her friend back. All the horror of the past would be wiped clean. She, Mercedes, wouldn't have been responsible for introducing her brother to his killer. She, Mercedes, would be guiltless of encouraging Rollo and his murderess to go out together. She, Mercedes, could at last unload her own sense of crushing guilt and find a life again.

Oriana sighed heavily. 'Logically, Mrs Greer's testimony can mean one of two things,' she explained patiently. 'One, I killed Rollo. Or two, I didn't kill Rollo, which means, ergo, that she was lying.'

Mercedes was dubious. It made no sense. Frances Greer, as far as Mercedes was aware, had nothing against Oriana. She had just been a friend of the daughter of the house.

'Look, Mercedes, I'm not asking you to trust me,' Oriana said, wishing she could reach out and grab her old friend's hand, but knowing that she couldn't. 'I'm not even asking you to believe me. I'm just asking you to help me.'

Mercedes laughed. It was a hard, grating sound, full of pain and disbelief. But, at the back of her mind, she was aware, once again, of that stirring of hope. 'Why should I?' she said bitterly. 'Can you give me one good reason why I should?'

Oriana smiled. 'Oh yes,' she said quickly. 'In fact, I can give you two.'

Mercedes took a shaky breath. 'Which are?'

'One. If I'm right, it means that your brother's killer is still out there somewhere, roaming around as free as a bird.' She didn't add that she was all but certain that she already knew who it was. 'And if you help me, there's the chance that you can help bring Rollo's murderer to justice.'

Mercedes licked her lips, which felt dry and cracked. 'And the second reason?' she croaked.

Oriana looked at her friend with compassion. 'Don't you want to know, Mercy? I mean, to be absolutely *certain*, once and for all?'

Mercedes looked away. She had been certain. Before Oriana came back, she'd had no doubts. But now . . . She sighed heavily. 'What do you want from me?' she asked quietly.

Oriana let her breath out in a quiet, relieved sigh. Until now, she hadn't realized how tense she'd been. 'I want you to think back to that summer. What had Rollo been doing? Was he excited about anything, or did he seem afraid of someone? He was still at university — did he ever tell you anything about Oxford? You see, we've got to find out the real motive for his murder.'

It was the one thing Oriana needed to know more than anything else. She knew *who*, but she didn't know *why*.

Mercedes was already shaking her head. 'He wasn't afraid of anybody,' she said with certainty. 'In fact, he seemed really upbeat. Kind of excited, now that I think about it. He had some sort of family project he was working on. He was really secretive about it, sort of chuffed, you know? Like he was keeping a wonderful surprise up his sleeve.' It was amazing, now that she let herself think about her brother's last few weeks, how much was coming back.

Oriana nodded. 'Yes. I noticed that, too. He was in a really good mood, for days and days. But what kind of family project was it?'

Mercedes shook her head. 'He didn't say. I only know he went to see Great-Aunt Agatha, up at Sunnyacres. What for, I don't know. He'd never bothered visiting her before, poor old thing. Although I'm a fine one to talk — I haven't been to see her for years myself. I must go and visit her one of these days.'

It didn't sound very promising. But it was all she had. Oriana sighed, then looked up as the kitchen door opened.

Connor walked in, bringing with him the smell of the outdoors and a healthy, male animal presence. His eyes immediately went to Mercedes. Not to Oriana, Mercedes noticed triumphantly, but to her.

'Hello, am I interrupting?' he asked, only then glancing across at his employer, an eyebrow raised in question.

Oriana smiled. 'No, we've just finished talking. Mercedes told me something helpful. About Rollo. We'll have to check it out.'

Mercedes got slowly to her feet. 'Well, I have to be off,' she said, hoping that Connor would do something. Anything.

He looked at her, his face gentle. 'I'll walk you home,' he said softly.

Mercedes' heart leapt, then she shot a thoughtful look at Oriana, but she was staring into her mug of tea, a small frown tugging at her brows. She didn't seem very possessive of him, did she? If Connor was hers, she'd certainly have something to say about him walking another woman home. 'OK, thanks,' Mercedes said brightly, and moved to join him. Together they left the kitchen.

'You look a bit washed out,' Connor said, as they walked slowly through the overgrown garden and out onto the lane. 'Rough, was it?' he asked sympathetically.

'Yes. It was rather,' she admitted. She looked up at him sharply. 'Connor, do you believe she did it?'

He knew the enormity of what she was asking. That she'd lived with the nightmare of her brother's murder by her best friend for almost all her adult life. She'd probably managed to grow a rough skin over it, a scab which had been pulled away with Oriana's return. Now she was confused again, and looking for reassurance. Guidance.

And she'd turned to him. Even knowing that he and Oriana were 'together'. Even knowing that he was in the enemy camp, she was still asking him, ready to believe and trust him. It made him swell with pride and happiness, yet ache with fear and wariness.

What if he'd got this all horribly wrong? Then he sighed heavily. 'If you're asking me what my instinct is,' he said carefully, 'then I'd say that Oriana no more killed your brother than the man in the moon. But if you're asking me to make your own mind up for you, forget it,' he said gruffly. Then added, with heart-stopping tenderness, 'Sweetheart, only you can do that.'

Mercedes flushed with pleasure, both because of what he was saying, and because of the endearment. *Sweetheart*. But it might mean nothing. It could be just a saying. Mercedes had had a cleaning lady once who called everyone 'my love'.

'It's my birthday party in two weeks' time,' she said softly. 'I want you to come. And Oriana, too,' she added, after a bare second's pause.

Connor, knowing what such a concession must have cost her, smiled and reached down, brushing the long black locks behind her ear. His huge hands easily dwarfed her oval face.

'I'll be there,' he promised.

* * *

In his conservatory, Fred Wright sprayed the tomato cuttings with a greenfly repellent. The pungent odour filled the glass house and, as he rolled his aching shoulders, he felt sweat trickle down his back. It was no good. He couldn't concentrate. Not even on his collection of rare orchids, usually his pride and joy.

He walked through into the hall, which felt incredibly cold after the moist heat of the conservatory, and shivered his way into the study. There he poured himself a brandy. On the table was the copy of the local paper which had robbed him of his sleep last night, and would probably rob him of his sleep tonight.

He picked it up once again, and read the blazing headline. STAIRCASE KILLER RETURNS TO SCENE OF HER CRIME

Underneath was a rather lurid but mostly accurate account of Rollo Seton's murder, and the trial which followed. The pictures accompanying it were of a sixteen-year-old Oriana Foster taken at the trial, and a new one, which had obviously been taken by an enterprising photo-journalist with a long-range camera lens, for it depicted Oriana working in the Manor's overgrown garden.

Did the villagers of Nether Dene really want a murderess living among them again, the article asked.

Fred threw the paper away and sat down in his chair. His arthritis was bothering him. He was old. His head hurt. He drank his brandy and stared at a painting above his fireplace. He wished he could persuade Margaret to come away with him somewhere. Take a long cruise of the Caribbean perhaps. Or go to Hawaii for a few months. But he knew she wouldn't come. She was too obsessed with Lowell Seton.

Fred was frightened. He was an old, frightened man.

On the floor in front of him, from the newsprint, Oriana's terrified sixteen-year-old face stared up at him accusingly. Fred began to cry.

* * *

Oriana pointed. 'There! That's got to be the turn-off.'

Connor grunted. 'It is. I can see the name on the sign.' Sunnyacres. They'd been driving for a little under an hour, and now, just across the border into Gloucestershire, he turned off the B road and onto a long, winding, private road set in acres of trees. The nursing home for the elderly was a dignified, exquisitely proportioned house which had once belonged to a country squire. The terrace which ran the length of its south-facing wall was peopled by old folk in wheelchairs.

Connor parked beneath the shade of a mighty horse chestnut, and together they walked into the office. A middle-aged woman, obviously a clerical worker, looked up, smiling a welcome. 'Hello,' Oriana said, smiling brightly. 'I was wondering if we could speak to Agatha Seton?'

The older woman, who'd been eyeing Connor with admiring surprise, turned to Oriana and smiled. 'My goodness, that's a name I haven't heard in a long time. I'm afraid Agatha's no longer with us. She died, oh, it must be three or four years ago now. She was one of our star residents – lived to get the telegram from the Queen,' she added significantly.

Oriana sighed heavily. She'd half expected it, of course. Still . . .

'Oh, what a shame,' Connor said, making Oriana's eyes widen – for he was speaking with a broad South African accent. 'I know Aunt Aggie was getting on, but I had no idea she was as old as all that. When Dad said we were to look her up and tell him how she was getting on, he never mentioned she might be gone. He will be disappointed – won't he, Shell?'

Oriana blinked. 'Oh, yes. Yes he will. What a pity,' she added, glad she'd already spoken so he wouldn't expect her to put on an accent too.

But Connor was already well away again. 'I don't suppose Aunt Aggie has any friends left here, does she? You know, someone we can talk to about the old days. I know how much Dad would like it if we could at least go back to Joburg and tell him her last years were happy ones. Perhaps with some pictures? A little memento?'

The secretary, looking sympathetic but flustered, was already shaking her head. 'Sorry, no. But the lady who always used to visit her here might be able to help you. I believe she used to be Mrs Seton's live-in housekeeper and companion. What was her name now . . . ?'

Five minutes later, Oriana and Connor were once more back on the road. Oriana, who still found travelling by car something of a thrill, wound down her passenger window and looked at Connor with amused eyes. She really must start taking driving lessons soon. 'Bit of a secret charmer, aren't you?' she teased mildly. 'You have middle-aged ladies eating out of your hand all the time?'

Connor grinned. 'Oh yes. Middle-aged ladies and dogs are a speciality. Even cats like me.'

Oriana could well believe it.

* * *

Mercedes was polishing the dog's silverware when she heard a light tap at her door.

'Come in,' she called out vaguely, not wanting the bother of getting up. The cleaner she was using had made her hands filthy, and she had cloths and cups all over the table. She never locked her door in the daytime, and when it opened and she heard footsteps, she'd half been expecting Lowell. Or maybe even Connor. So when she looked up and saw Oriana, her face fell.

Oriana smiled wryly. 'Hello again, Mercy,' she said. 'Sorry to bother you so soon. I wouldn't be here if it wasn't important.'

Mercedes managed a small smile. 'That's OK. Take a chair.'

Funny, but less than a week ago, if somebody had told her that Oriana Foster would be sitting at her table, and that Mercedes herself would be – almost – easy about having her there, she'd have thought they were out of their mind. 'Sorry I can't get you anything,' she said, holding out her hands. 'But as you can see . . .'

Oriana nodded. 'It's fine.' She craned her neck sideways to read one of the cups and a fair eyebrow rose in surprise. 'Dog shows?'

'Boxers. I breed them. Make a very good living at it, actually,' Mercedes said.

Oriana laughed. 'You always did like dogs. I'm glad. That you're doing well, I mean.'

Mercedes nodded, and an awkward silence fell.

If Oriana had looked out the window, she would have seen Lowell, a few hundred yards away, leaving the Manor and crossing the gravel car park, towards the connecting gate which led to Mercedes' Honeysuckle Cottage. By the time he was walking up the garden path, Mercedes was at the sink, washing her hands.

'I'll just look up one of my old address books,' she said now to Oriana, after she'd given Mercedes the sad news about her great-aunt and relayed the details of their visit. 'I think Aunt Agatha's housekeeper should be in it. She was very fond of Agatha, for some reason. Don't know why – she

79

always treated poor old Miss Ford like a doormat.' She left the tiny kitchen and went through to the drawing room. She thought she saw a passing shadow as she bent down to rummage around in her odds-and-ends drawer, but when she straightened up, the address book in hand, there was no one at the window. She shrugged and went back to the kitchen. 'Yes, here it is,' she said, and reaching for the notebook she usually kept for jotting down her grocery lists, copied out Miss Ford's address in the nearby town of Brackley.

'Mind you, I don't know if she's still there,' Mercedes said, handing over the scrap of paper. Oriana stood up and put it in her jeans pocket.

'Thanks a lot,' she said. At that moment, the door opened and Lowell walked in.

* * *

Margaret Wright parked her car in front of the Dower House Hotel and walked in, heading for Lowell's office.

* * *

Oriana stared at Lowell helplessly. After freezing for a bare second, he walked slowly in and closed the door – with ominous calm – behind him.

'It seems I can't go anywhere without you haunting my every footstep,' he said gruffly. He glanced quizzically at Mercedes, who shook her head helplessly.

'I've got to go see to the dogs,' she murmured, and turned and quickly fled through the French doors which led out into the back garden.

Oriana felt her heart flutter nervously. 'I could say the same thing about you,' she said at last.

Lowell smiled grimly. He was dressed in his usual working suit of deep dark blue, white shirt and, today, ice-blue tie. He looked devastatingly handsome. He'd been devastating enough at the tender age of sixteen. Now taller, filled out, and with years of experience and living behind him, he was more, much more, than she could cope with.

'I'd better go,' she said, her voice cracking with tension.

* * *

Margaret Wright left the reception desk, frowning. He hadn't left a message. Where the hell was Lowell? It was only four o'clock; he couldn't have finished work already. She knew, to her cost, what a workaholic he was. Some nights she had to literally drag him from his office. She stood, looking around, and spotted his car. He'd not taken it then. She nodded, smiling in sudden satisfaction. There was only one place he could possibly be. She, too, turned and headed for Honeysuckle Cottage.

* * *

'Oh, don't rush off on my account,' Lowell said, his sarcasm making Oriana flinch. 'After all, it's a free country.'

Oriana took it. From Lowell, even pain was better than absence. She'd had thirteen years without him. Now, even his scorn, even his hate, felt like nectar.

'Lowell,' she said, but he held up a hand.

'Please, spare me,' he said harshly. 'I don't know what you said to Mercy to make her listen, but don't try it on me.'

It was another hot day outside, and the windows were wide open. In the distance, she thought she heard the latch on the gate lift and reconnect.

'Lowell,' she said again, restlessly moving from foot to foot. 'Please.'

'Please what?' he said savagely.

Oriana shook her head. 'Lowell, I didn't kill Rollo. And I intend to prove it. Can't you just . . . hold on?' she whispered. Her big blue eyes pleaded with him.

Lowell stared at her, horrified, because he could feel himself giving way. Was he insane? Had the last thirteen wretched years taught him nothing?

He was fourteen when he'd first become truly aware of Oriana Foster. For all that they'd gone to school together, that Oriana and Mercedes had been joined at the hip, it was three days after his fourteenth birthday that he'd actually *noticed* her.

She and Mercy had been in the apple orchard, collecting windfalls for Mrs Greer to bake into pies and crumbles. It was September, and a sudden shower had sent the two girls scurrying and laughing into the hall. He'd been coming down the stairs, and Oriana had stopped in the hall, shaking herself free of raindrops like a dog. Her damp curls had been longer then, bouncing around her shoulders. She'd laughed, caught sight of him, and looked up.

And Lowell had fallen in love. Aged fourteen. On the stairs, in his old home.

Since then, he'd done nothing but dream of her. One way or another. To begin with, it had been wonderful. First love. He didn't let her know, of course, content, boy-like, to worship from afar. A year came and went. And then she began to go out with Rollo. He was crushed. Devastated. Until he began to suspect why she was doing it. Whenever they were together, it was to him, Lowell, that her eyes would stray. It had been wonderful, blissful, to know that she thought of him, too.

He'd made up his mind to tell Rollo that he couldn't have her. Even though, at nineteen, Rollo had been so much the older brother, Lowell was determined to fight him for her. And then the unthinkable happened.

To this day, Lowell didn't know what the argument had been about which had made Oriana push him down the stairs. But he suspected. Oh yes, he suspected, all right. And the knowledge crippled him. Because it had to have been about him.

Rollo had found out that Oriana really wanted Lowell. And Rollo wouldn't have stood for that. It would have hurt his pride to have his little brother beat him in the romance stakes. Even at sixteen, Lowell had sensed that Rollo was jealous of him. He'd always been better at school, and now he'd heard people say how much better-looking than his older brother he was. In his darker moments, he'd wondered if Rollo had taunted Oriana, or even attacked her, giving her no choice but to fight back. And that made him feel even more guilty – that he could be so disloyal to his own flesh and blood.

And now here Oriana was again. Back in his life. Still protesting her innocence. Still turning him, effortlessly, inside out. But Lowell didn't dare believe her, because he'd wanted, yearned, prayed for so long and so desperately for her to be innocent. Because if she hadn't done it then it meant that he, too, was innocent.

'I'm going to find out what really happened, Lowell,' Oriana said, loudly and clearly, dragging him back from the yawning, nightmare precipice. 'With or without you, I'm going to find out what really happened that night.'

We'll be all right, you and me, her eyes promised. *Soon, everything will be all right. Just hold on. Oh, my love, just hold on.*

Outside, Margaret Wright froze. Then she came closer, pulling aside a swathe of climbing honeysuckle from the window-frame, and looked in.

Lowell stared at Oriana with blazing eyes. Could it really be true? Could she really be innocent? He took a step towards her. He thought she was moving too. She was so pale, so lovely. Her big blue eyes were like magnets.

Suddenly, she was in his arms. He had no idea how she'd got there. Who had moved first? Did it matter? Gloriously, for the first time she was in his arms. He'd waited so long for this moment, with absolutely no hope of it ever happening. Dreading it. Wanting it. Living for it. Feeling himself die a little every day because it wasn't happening.

But now it was. She felt warm, hard and yet soft. The smell of violets was in her hair.

'Oh, Lowell,' Oriana cried, lifting her face to his.

With a groan, Lowell's lips swooped onto hers. He wanted to absorb her, to take her into himself, to cast out, once and for all, the demons of the last thirteen years. His body, for the first time, flamed into life. He felt himself throbbing against her, and understood how desperately he wanted her. Knew, too, that in another moment – just one more incredibly lovely moment – she'd have him. Mind, body and soul.

And he wouldn't care.

With a muffled cry he thrust her away from him. Oriana stumbled back against the table, her face ashen, her blue eyes blazing. She held out a hand, but he was already turning away, staggering a little, as he lunged into the hall and was gone.

* * *

Outside, Margaret Wright watched him walk blindly back towards the hotel. Her eyes were dark with rage.

Inside, Oriana slowly lowered herself into a chair, and burst into sobs. She didn't know whether they were tears of happiness or tears of pain.

Perhaps, for her, they would always be the same.

SEVEN

Oriana watched as Connor pressed the doorbell. Miss G.J. Ford, one-time housekeeper/companion to Mercedes' Great-Aunt Agatha, lived in a modest semi-detached house on one of Brackley's bigger housing estates. The garden was neat but uninspired, and something about the estate depressed her.

The door opened and Oriana moved a step forward. She and Connor hadn't been able to agree just how to approach Miss Ford. Oriana was for telling the simple truth, but Connor, more wise and experienced perhaps, had argued that Miss Ford was likely to slam the door in their faces if they did. He preferred a cover – perhaps as reporters. They'd argued good-naturedly about it on the drive over, but the moment Miss Ford saw Oriana, it was obvious that the argument had been settled for them.

She was a small woman, as neat as her garden, dressed in a tweed suit complete with fake pearls. Her curly grey hair had recently been permed. But it was the expression on her face which instantly set Oriana's heart racing. For it was fear. Sheer, simple fear. Then, the next moment, Oriana felt sick as she realized just why Miss G.J. Ford was frightened. She was frightened of Oriana.

Oriana took an instinctive step back, her hand going to her mouth, an appalled look racing to her face. Fool! She should have known that Miss Ford would regard the murder of Rollo, a great-nephew of her employer, as a major event in her life. She'd probably read the newspaper reports of the trial avidly, and seen the photographs of Oriana which had accompanied them.

Connor shifted restlessly, no doubt coming to all the same conclusions she had, and the old lady turned to look at him. Unfortunately, his size only made her even more scared. Just as she was scuttling backwards, about to slam the door in her face, Connor spoke.

'Do I have the pleasure of addressing Miss Ford?' he said, his accent so upper crust it could have stopped a cart horse at a hundred paces. It stopped Miss Ford in her tracks. 'Miss G.J. Ford, formerly of Cedar Acres, Upper Westcott?' Connor sounded as if he'd just stepped out of Buckingham Palace, or off the pages of *Tatler*. To someone of Miss Ford's generation and previous employment, it must have sounded like a lifeline.

She flushed, utterly bemused. 'Yes. I am she,' she said stiffly, unconsciously echoing Connor's precise grammar.

'Ah, then please allow me to introduce myself.' He leaned into his jacket pocket and produced a card. Oriana watched, fascinated but still appalled. That she could inspire fear in someone was sickening to her.

'Mr Grantham P. Fortescue. Of Lowestoft and Fortescue,' Connor added, smiling briefly. It was a charming smile; even Oriana, who only caught its side features, could see that. 'Solicitors,' Connor added. And left so much unsaid. Solicitors to the gentry. Solicitors for centuries. Only deeds and wills and other such respectable undertakings preferred. Nothing criminal. Nothing nasty. Oh no.

'Oh,' Miss Ford said, understanding as well as anybody (and better than most) all those unsaid but *understood* things. She glanced once more at Oriana, wondering if she had made a mistake. Obviously a gentleman like Mr Fortescue would have nothing to do with something, or someone, as common as a criminal.

'This is Miss Oriana Foster, a client of our establishment,' Connor carried on. 'Miss Foster finds herself in a very unfortunate situation. We at Lowestoft and Fortescue are convinced that she was the victim of a heinous miscarriage of justice, and we believe that you, Miss Ford, can help us. Perhaps we could take you out to lunch somewhere and discuss it? I'm afraid I don't know this area very well – were we in Oxford I could of course take you to Browns, or the Randolph. Er, perhaps you know of some quiet, refined place nearby?'

The fact that he wasn't asking to be let in, and was familiar with the famous Browns, and the equally five-star Randolph in Oxford, decided Miss Ford on the spot as no amount of flimflam could have done.

'Oh please, do come in. I have tea. Chinese or Indian?'

She didn't look at Oriana, and the younger woman followed her into a small kitchen still feeling sick at heart. Within minutes, however, Connor had her at her ease. He was dressed, luckily, in a charcoal suit from a bespoke tailor from Osney, but when he helped her with a flimsy little tea tray, he still looked touchingly absurd. Nevertheless, Miss Ford was soon chatting to him like a long-lost son. So at ease was she that when Connor slowly turned the talk towards Rollo Seton, Miss Ford evinced no signs of distress.

Oriana was more than willing to leave all the questioning to Connor. When she'd hired her bodyguard, she'd had no idea she was also buying such a first-rate con artist as well! But then, he hadn't batted an eyelid when she asked him to pose as her boyfriend, so she figured he might be rather used to adopting personas.

'Oh yes, poor boy. Agatha was very fond of him. Although, I must say, I always thought Lowell was her favourite. He had the brains, she used to say. And the looks.'

'But Rollo was the one who visited her in Sunnyacres, I believe?' Connor said, politely interested.

'No, I don't think so,' Miss Ford negated. 'I remember her saying that Mercedes came to see her a few times. But . . . Oh! Wait, now that you mention it, she did say Rollo had come to talk to her. And about such an odd thing, too. Agatha was quite surprised to find him so interested. I mean, it was such a long time ago. Although, I suppose, being a young man, it was the thought of gambling which had attracted his attention so. Although where he'd heard the story, I couldn't say.'

Oriana, who hadn't dared pick up her own cup of tea, felt her already cold hands begin to tremble in her lap, and she held them together tightly. She cast Connor a quick, urgent look, but she needn't have worried. He was already ahead of her.

'Gambling? Oh dear, I hope he didn't get into difficulties. Some young men, even from the best of families, can get themselves into an awful mess. I remember the youngest son of the Marquis of . . . oh, but I mustn't, of course, name names. Even though I'm sure I could rely on *your* discretion, Miss Ford,' he said, green eyes twinkling.

Miss Ford blossomed. 'Oh well, of course,' she said, obviously fascinated to find out which young lordling had been up to no good. Then she recalled herself. She had her old mistress's family reputation to protect!

'Oh no, it was nothing of that kind,' she said quickly. 'I'm talking now about a famous poker game which Agatha's brother, Rollo's great-grandfather, had once indulged in, many, many years ago. Rollo had come to ask her about it. Agatha said the lad was utterly fascinated by it.'

Connor nodded. 'Yes, I see,' he said, obviously not seeing at all. 'Was it a large sum of money which changed hands?'

'Oh no, I don't think so. The Setons weren't cash rich back then. I believe it was land which changed hands,' Miss Ford said casually.

'So Rollo wanted to know how much land was lost?' Connor probed.

'Oh no. Not *lost*,' Miss Ford said, with second-hand pride. 'Won. Apparently, old Bartholomew Seton won quite a few acres off Ebeneezer Usted. Agatha wasn't sure where the land was, though. Or if the Setons still owned it. Perhaps that was why Rollo was so interested; what with his father dying and having inheritance tax to pay, I suppose he thought he might want to sell it off.'

'Ah, yes,' Connor said. 'That would be it. The bane of our life at Lowestoft and Fortescue, I can tell you. Inheritance tax,' he said, shaking his head.

Miss Ford's prim lips tightened in sympathy, and together, for a while, they mutually deplored that avaricious penalty.

Oriana was quiet on the way home. Connor was glad – it gave him a chance to mull over what they'd learned. Like Oriana, he'd found the tale fascinating, but also like Oriana, he couldn't see how such an old poker game could lead to Rollo's murder.

'Can you drop me off in Oxford?' Oriana said, as they hit the motorway. 'I want to do some research in the library. Find out what I can about this land which changed hands.' Ebeneezer Usted was such an unusual name, she'd surely be able to find some trace of him in the local history section.

'Sure,' Connor said. After he'd dropped Oriana off, he went to a small delicatessen he knew, just off St Aldates, and filled a basket before driving back to Nether Dene. Getting out of the car, however, he turned away from the Manor and walked briskly down Church Lane instead, towards Honeysuckle Cottage. Walking past banks of lupins and delphiniums, snapdragons and peonies, he reached the door.

Mercedes looked satisfyingly pleased to see him. He smiled and held up his shopping bag. 'Hello. I thought I might persuade you to come for a picnic,' he said cheerfully.

Mercedes' smile widened. 'I know just the place.'

The Lasher was a long weir built across a small mill race, cut out from the River Cherwell when the old mill had been a working granary. Now it was overgrown with flowering water-crowfoot, and, they soon discovered, a nesting pair of kingfishers who were at first wary of their presence, but soon grew accustomed to them. As they darted to and from the riverbank, flashes of turquoise and orange, Mercedes and Connor watched them from the shade of a weeping willow. In the meadow behind them, Hereford cows grazed contentedly and, to the music of the river splashing and racing down the weir, the wind added its own susurration. Banks of rosebay willowherb moved in the breeze, a pink curtain of flowers, cutting them off from view of the cows, and any passing ramblers or fishermen.

'Hmm, that was wonderful,' Mercedes said, leaning back on Connor's spread jacket. They'd had no blanket, and she felt a bit worried about sitting down on his obviously expensive jacket, but he'd insisted. She'd smiled and called him a modern-day Walter Raleigh, and he'd grinned enigmatically.

When he'd opened the shopping bag, revealing pâté de foie gras, delicious smoked salmon canapes, red grapes still with the bloom on them, a piece of brie, fresh crusty loaves still warm from an oven, and a bottle of champagne, she'd been speechless. She understood now why he'd asked her to get a knife and some glasses.

Now, the food consumed, the champagne all but gone, she watched the clouds floating by above her, utterly replete. Connor watched her with sleepy but masculine-hungry eyes. She was dressed in a simple summer frock of bright orange, with white daisies linking in chains across the fabric. She'd shaken her long black hair free of its ponytail, and now, trailing across the green grass, she looked a vision of colour and beauty. Vibrant and feminine. He knew many people would consider Oriana, of the two of them, to be the most classically beautiful, but to Connor, Mercedes was someone special.

He liked everything about her. Her eyes. Her smile. Her dogs. Her cottage. Her garden. Her fit, young body. Her courage. It had taken guts, and a generosity of spirit, to invite Oriana to her birthday party, and Connor didn't know another woman who would have done it. And he also knew, in his heart of hearts, that she'd done it for him. Because she knew it was what he wanted.

She looked over at him, and big hazel irises watched him speculatively. He wondered if his face had been as naked as his thoughts, and he slowly lay down beside her. Mercedes watched him move, once again thrilled and fascinated by the way he could move such a big body so fluidly. He always moved silently. She realized, with a start, that she knew nothing about him. At all.

'What do you do for a living?' she asked, turning on her side to rest her cheek against her forearm. He reached out and idly traced the line of her nose. Her lips. Her chin.

He sighed. 'I run my own company.' He hoped she wouldn't ask what kind. If it got out what he really did for a living, it might blow Oriana's cover and alert the real killer to the fact that she was protected by a professional. He didn't want that, which meant, if Mercedes asked, he'd have to lie. And he wanted to do that even less. Something in his tone must have alerted her, for she abruptly changed the subject.

'Not married? Or ever been?'

Connor smiled. 'No.'

'Not gay?'

Connor grinned. 'No.'

'Tell me about yourself,' she said, snuggling closer. 'It's like pulling teeth getting information from you.'

And so Connor told her. His parents dying young and being raised by a grandmother, also now dead. Life in a London suburb. School. The army. Not too much about what he did in the army, but Mercedes didn't need to be told. Now she understood the silence of his movements, the fitness of that huge body and the ever-present alertness in the eyes. She didn't ask him if he'd ever had to kill anyone during his days as a soldier, either. She already knew.

As Connor swept on, telling her about leaving the army, putting his pay and savings to good use, starting a one-man outfit, building it up, always alone and independent, he realized that nothing he'd said had scared her. Not the harshness of his early career. Not his lifestyle now. Not even the fact that he was the live-in lover (supposedly) of Oriana Foster. Nothing scared her. It made him feel both humble and grateful. When he'd finished, he reached out and pushed tendrils of long black hair from her face.

'Your turn,' he whispered.

Mercedes reached for a tress of his longish, straw-coloured hair, and twisted it gently between her fingers. 'You already know everything,' she said matter-of-factly. 'You know my life history. What else can I add, except the fact that I've had three lovers. None satisfactory, and none lately.' She took a deep breath, and perhaps the biggest chance of her life. 'And none like you.'

Connor stared for a long while into her hazel eyes, then he leaned over and kissed her: long, hard, tenderly, passionately.

Mercedes rolled over onto her back, her hands on his shoulders, pulling him with her. He went willingly – she'd certainly never have been able to move him otherwise – taking his weight on his bent elbows. With his free hand he roamed her body, along her waist, down her thigh, back to her waist, his splayed hand easily covering the width and depth of her flat stomach. Then up, to cup her breast. He lifted his lips to let her take a breath, and heard her draw in a sweet, needy gasp.

She opened her eyes. 'It's just a little too soon,' she heard herself say. And could have kicked herself.

Connor nodded. 'That's all right,' he said softly. 'I'm in no hurry.' He smiled tenderly. 'At least not now.'

* * *

Back in the village, Oriana got off the bus and walked through the near-deserted village to the Manor House. She met only two people – one old man walking his dog, a man she vaguely remembered from her childhood as being a gardener and odd-job man. He nodded to her pleasantly enough, but the second person, a middle-aged woman Oriana had never met, looked at her with a curious mixture of nervousness and contempt.

Oriana didn't really relax until she was back home. There she found a large buff envelope waiting for her along with the other mail, and her heart did a small leap. It was from her firm of private investigators. Quickly she ripped it open and extracted the report. She read avidly for five minutes, relaxing even more with every word she read. When she was finished, she nodded. It made sense. She had a wonderful sensation of everything coming together at last. She was beginning to see daylight at the end of the long, dark, lonely tunnel, and after the day she'd had, it was even more welcome.

Another piece of the jigsaw puzzle fitted. Now, if only she could tie up the real killer to the latest piece, she would soon be able to take her findings to her solicitor. Then, through him, to the police. She didn't know, exactly, what she'd have to do to earn herself a full pardon, but now, for the first time, she had something more than hope and determination to make her believe that one day she'd get there.

* * *

If Oriana was in a good mood, Mercedes was in an even better one. As she pushed open her garden gate, she turned to Connor, about to invite him in, to tell him that she'd changed her mind. Why wait? She knew he was the one.

She'd changed the sheets, and would perhaps ask him to share her shower – it would be interesting to see how such a big man would fill up the space in her tiny bathroom. They could spend the afternoon making love, then afterwards she could— She looked up, her mouth opening, only to find Connor staring over her shoulder. He looked . . . not grim, exactly, but more resigned.

She looked behind her and saw Lowell. He'd obviously been inside the house, perhaps coming over to invite her to lunch. Now he walked up the garden path, his face set in stone. He walked stiffly, obviously fighting back some strong emotion, and Mercedes felt all her own happiness slowly leach away.

Connor looked down at Mercedes, and saw her face tighten. He sighed heavily. 'I'll see you soon,' he said clearly. Then he squeezed her hand and was gone. It was no part of his brief to get into a fight, verbal or otherwise, with Lowell Seton. He had to remember that although he was undoubtedly falling for Mercedes, it was still Oriana who was the client. And, as such, deserved his best efforts on her behalf.

Lowell watched the big man disappear up the road, then looked at his sister.

'I hope to hell you know what you're doing,' he said bleakly. And then he wondered. Why should she? He had no idea what he was doing, after all. Why should his sister be any different?

Mercedes' eyes flashed a warning. 'Leave it, Lowell,' she said softly. 'Connor's none of your business.'

No, he thought grimly. He wasn't. He was just living with the woman he loved.

Hated.

Loved.

He shook his head and leaned tiredly against the gate. He was going to have to get his life in order. First, sort things out with Margaret. He'd let their relationship, if it could be called that, wander along like a lost sheep. It wasn't fair to her. He'd have to tell her it was all over between them. Then he'd get on to the new owners of the Manor, make a firm offer. Then . . .

Wordlessly, Mercedes put a hand on his shoulder. It felt extremely tense. He looked at her questioningly. She bit her lip, wondering if she should speak. But then, there'd been so many years of silence. Perhaps it was time. 'You love her, don't you?' she said quietly.

Lowell's head shot up, his face pale, grey eyes blazing. He shook his head vigorously. But he meant yes. They both knew that.

'I thought so,' Mercedes said. 'Ever since you were a boy, huh?'

Lowell nodded.

'Perhaps she really didn't do it,' she said at last. 'Did you ever think of that?'

Lowell laughed grimly. 'Only every minute of every day. Followed by the certainty that she did do it. Followed by the thought that it was all my fault. Followed by the hope that she'd die in prison, so I'd never have to see her again. Followed by the promise that, with every day which passed, she was a step nearer to being free, where I *could* see her. Followed by the thought that . . . oh what the hell's the use?' he said bleakly.

Mercedes felt her throat close up. She'd known that Lowell had been unhappy all these years, like herself, but she hadn't realized until now just how *desperately* unhappy he'd been. No wonder he was always exhausted, living like that – so hopelessly torn. It would have destroyed many another man. But not Lowell. He was made of granite. Which was just as well, considering.

'Go and see her, Lowell,' Mercedes said. 'Talk to her. Or listen to her. But try and . . . do *something*. Before it's too late. Before we all explode and destroy everything that's left.'

It was some minutes before Lowell realized that his sister was gone. He straightened, walked stiffly through the gate, then hesitated.

To one side stood the Dower House Hotel; his work – his life, such as it was. To the other side stood the Manor House, his old home – and Oriana.

Only one thing seemed real.

* * *

Oriana looked up, expecting Connor, her smile faltering as Lowell walked into the room. She was sitting in the main living room, the investigator's report on the scarred wooden coffee table in front of her, colour charts and decorating

95

magazines on the other. She got to her feet slowly. Lowell raised his hands in a gesture of appeasement. 'Pax,' he said, the word taking him straight back to his childhood when he, Mercedes, and sometimes Rollo, would play chase in the orchard.

Oriana, too, remembered, and for a moment her eyes flooded with tears. Then she smiled and nodded. 'Pax,' she agreed, sinking back down onto the sofa. Her knees weren't even as strong as jelly.

He brought into the room with him not only his extraordinary male beauty, but also a sense of power, of life. For how long, Oriana wondered, with a mixture of bleak pleasure, had Lowell meant life itself to her?

Lowell moved forward, glancing down at the magazines. 'So you really are an interior designer?'

Oriana blinked. What? Then she remembered her cover story and followed his eyes to the magazines. She'd only been looking through them for some preliminary ideas. She'd intended to hire a local firm later to see about transforming the Manor. It was such a lovely old house, and had been unloved for far too long.

'Can I sit down?' he asked.

Oriana jerked her hand helplessly. 'Of course you can,' she said, watching as he lowered himself into an overstuffed armchair. His jacket was off, his tie stuffed haphazardly into a pocket. She remembered the touch of his lips on hers, and wanted it again, fiercely. So much, in fact, that she could actually feel her lips ache.

'You've turned my life upside down,' Lowell said slowly. 'But then, I suppose you know that?'

Oriana swallowed hard. 'That wasn't my intention.'

'No. Your intention was to prove your innocence. Is that right? Or have you changed your mind?'

Oriana shook her head. 'No, I haven't changed my mind. And today, I'm one step closer.'

She saw the flash of hope ignite in his eyes, then slowly bank down as mentally he argued against it. But at least the hope *had* been there, she told herself, her heart pounding. That meant, didn't it, that at least he *wanted* it to be true? That was something. Oh yes, that was something. More than enough to set her heart singing again.

'Yes. One step nearer to proving the truth,' she continued, with deceiving calm, for her only chance of happiness lay in proving her innocence to Lowell, and she was well aware of the odds still stacked against her. 'Do you remember Frances Greer, Lowell? The housekeeper who so conveniently told the court that it was me who pushed Rollo? Do you know what happened to her after the trial?'

She couldn't keep the bitterness from her voice and didn't even try. 'Shall I tell you what happened to her, Lowell? She moved to Brighton, that's what happened to her. And bought herself a nice big bungalow on the coast. Now wasn't that nice for her?'

Lowell stared at her, at first distracted by her tone of voice. He'd never known her sound so hard before. So sardonic. Then, slowly, her words penetrated. 'What do you mean? What has that got to do with anything?'

Oriana smiled. It wasn't a nice smile. 'Don't you wonder where good old Frances Greer got the money from, Lowell?' she asked, almost tauntingly. 'After all, she was your housekeeper, wasn't she? Did you pay her a fortune in wages? Did she miraculously win the lottery? Did some convenient relative just up and die, perhaps, and leave her enough money to retire to Brighton? And just after the trial too. Doesn't that strike you as odd, Lowell?'

Lowell flushed. 'It sure as hell does,' he snapped, then added grimly, 'if it's true.'

Oriana smiled. 'Oh, it's true. And, what's more, I intend to find out just where that money came from.' She was going to telephone her investigators tonight and tell them to make that their next priority. They'd done a good job in locating Frances Greer, and she only hoped they'd make as good a job chasing the money trail. She didn't care who they had to bribe, she needed to be able to prove who'd paid her off.

Who'd paid her to lie.

Lowell stared at Oriana, fascinated. His heart, for some reason, was tripping, hard and heavy in his chest. The air was thick with tension. Sexual tension. He knew he had to get out of there. Quick. Before he did something he'd regret.

He got up slowly, and so did she. For a long moment, they stared at each other. And for the first time Oriana saw something other than hate or despair in his eyes. Desire. Confusion, too. Her eyes flared, and she took a quick step towards him. Then she froze as he turned and left.

But he'd be back. For the first time, she was sure. He'd be back.

Oriana thrust her clenched fist into the air, a triumphant but silent *Yes!* ringing in her mind. Lowell was going to be hers. As he always should have been hers.

* * *

Outside, Margaret Wright turned off onto Church Lane but suddenly hit the brakes, for she had spotted Lowell leaving the Manor House, head down and almost running. Even from this distance, she could fairly feel the emotion oozing out of him. Coming at her in waves. And she knew there was only one person who could make Lowell *feel* so much.

All her life, Margaret had had it all. Looks, money, power. Now one little upstart jailbird was trying to take what she'd marked out for her own.

Hah!

Margaret watched Lowell lope away. He was so beautiful. So young and fit. And mentally desirable too. He was no mere toyboy to be played with and tossed aside, like so many other men she'd had in her life. She'd quickly discovered that much. There was depth behind that stunningly handsome face. Oceans of it.

No, she would never let him go. She just wouldn't.

Which meant she'd have to get rid of Oriana Foster.

EIGHT

Lowell parked outside the small detached house just off Headington Hill and turned off the ignition. He sat and gazed at the house for a few moments, a puzzled frown on his brooding face. Then he checked the slip of paper on the passenger seat opposite him once more.

It was definitely the right address.

Lowell had used up quite a few hours and plenty of favours that morning, and then had spent even more time chasing paper trails, but he'd eventually tracked down the offices of OxonCountryProp Developments. But the house was an obvious residence, so presumably Marcus Royle was a one-man outfit who worked from home. Odd, surely, for a company which could afford to buy the Manor outright, and pay for conversion costs and a private interior designer?

It didn't add up.

He got out of the car and walked to the door, glancing around the deserted streets. Suburbia at its most inoffensive. Even the big tabby cat which sat on the wall opposite watched him from a polite distance.

The door opened a bare few seconds after his initial knock, and Lowell found himself facing a middle-aged man, with neatly cut greying hair and wide horn-rimmed glasses.

He looked like a typical accountant. Hardly the go-getting head of a major real-estate company.

'Hello, Mr Royle?'

The eyes smiled, crinkling attractively into crow's feet at the corners. 'Yes?'

'Of OxonCountryProp Developments?'

The smile vanished at once, to be replaced by a nervous blink. 'Er . . . sorry?'

'You are Mr Royle? You *do* own OxonCountryProp Developments?' Lowell persisted.

Marcus Royle looked more nervous than ever. 'I'm not sure . . .' he began, rather helplessly, and Lowell moved a step forward, forcing him back.

'My name's Lowell Seton,' he said briskly. 'My family used to own the Manor at Nether Dene. I've come to make you an offer for it,' he carried on firmly, all but shouldering his way into the small hall.

He already knew that Marcus Royle was going to present him with no serious problem. In his life, Lowell had dealt with fearsome bank managers, irate American multi-millionaires with complaints about the Dower House Hotel, not to mention reporters with all the charm and panache of Rottweilers on steroids. All of them had come off worst, quickly learning that behind the classically handsome face and polite English country gentleman persona lurked a man of utter steel. The likes of poor Marcus Royle were no challenge at all.

Less than a quarter of an hour later, Lowell left, grim-faced and bemused, but much, much the wiser.

As he got in the car and drove home, his mind was spinning. Oriana was the true owner of the Manor? But how could that be? Not that he doubted Marcus Royle's story for one moment. It was too fantastic to be a lie. And, in some sort of way, he was sure it made sense. If he could only figure it out. Which, on the face of it, seemed impossible. Where did she get the money? When she was convicted she was only sixteen. Could her aunt have died and left her money? But how? The cottage she'd lived in was rented. She had no other property, let alone the kind of money it must have taken to buy the Manor.

And you couldn't earn a fortune inside. Unless Oriana had somehow fallen in with a rich crook. But that was even more absurd. Had she won the lottery? Fantastic. Besides, he was almost sure prisoners weren't allowed to buy lottery tickets, and her purchase of the Manor must have been done almost on leaving the prison itself. It had the distinct air of a well-planned campaign about it.

So where did the money come from?

Into Lowell's mind came Oriana's news about Frances Greer, who had also mysteriously come into money. Enough to retire to Brighton and buy a property there. But the money couldn't have come from the same source, could it? Would someone really bribe another person to commit perjury, get an innocent woman convicted, then turn around and give the injured party enough money to be able to buy the Manor.

Come to that, just how much money *did* Oriana have?

Lowell pulled out to overtake a tractor, then slowed down instinctively as his mind continued to twist and turn. Was it possible that someone had paid Oriana to take the rap? But no. What sixteen-year-old girl would agree to be convicted of murder? Even if you could somehow orchestrate the trial, it made no sense. But there was obviously something going on that Oriana hadn't told him about. And he intended to find out what it was.

It wasn't until he got home that he realized he was now taking it for granted that Oriana was innocent. It shocked him enough to make him literally stagger from the car. He stood for a long, long moment, clinging onto the open car door for support.

Was Oriana innocent? And what did it mean to him if she was? The thought was enough to make his head spin and his heart do somersaults.

* * *

Mercedes picked up the phone and hesitated. What if Connor wasn't home? What if Oriana answered? What if she was making a big mistake? Oh hell, what if a big meteor hit the earth tomorrow and wiped everyone out? She dialled the number and waited.

'Hello?'

Her heart leapt at the sound of his voice. 'Hello, it's me. How about coming over for a late lunch? I've made spaghetti.'

What if he didn't like spaghetti?

'Sounds too good to be true. Give me ten seconds,' Connor said, then he hung up and ran, very fast, down the road. It was, in fact, twenty-two seconds before he knocked on her door, but Mercedes, who'd actually been counting, decided to let him off. She opened the door with a smile, wearing a long plastic apron with the picture of a bottle of beer on it, and very little else.

Connor eyed her long bare legs, slender bare arms and smiled.

'Who needs celebrity chefs when a man can come home to you?' he said gruffly, ushering her inside. When she turned around, presenting him with her back, he could make out a pair of very short turquoise shorts and a skimpy halterneck top.

The kitchen table was set with a red-and-white check tablecloth, complete with a candle in an empty wine bottle. On the stove simmered a tomato sauce which fragranced the tiny room with mouth-watering possibilities. Connor opened the bottle of chilled white wine she put on the table, and watched her ladle out the meal.

'Cheers,' she said softly, clinking glasses over the steaming plates.

'Special occasion?' Connor asked, mint-green eyes softening as she pushed back a long strand of black hair.

'Sort of,' she said nervously.

Connor felt his big heart begin to pick up the beat. His body began to harden. He forced himself to take a long, slow breath. 'Anything I should know about?' he asked, gruffly, his throat dry.

Mercedes smiled. 'Well, it does *involve* you,' she said, eyes twinkling, thinking of the pristine sheets upstairs, waiting on her bed.

And on the scented candle she'd lit in her small bedroom. 'I've changed my mind,' she said bravely.

'A lady's privilege,' Connor said promptly. Then, almost purring, 'About what, exactly?'

Mercedes met his eyes without flinching. 'About waiting.'

Connor was already on his feet by the time she'd uttered the last syllable. He moved around the table, making her look up – and up – at him, then he was reaching down and literally hooking her from the chair. He carried her as if she weighed nothing more than a feather pillow and headed for the narrow, twisting stairs. He had to duck, almost double, to get under the bend in the stairs, and she felt her long hair sweep against the bare wooden boards of the steps. Her heart was beating like a trapped bird in her chest, and her nipples, already hard, ached as they brushed against the side of his arm and the middle of his chest.

'That door,' she said, indicating the cottage's main bedroom.

Inside, the scent of jasmine and honeysuckle greeted them, and Connor, his eyes lighting up with relief at the sight of a big double bed, gently laid her squarely in the middle. Holding her eyes with his, he stood back and slipped off his shirt. Her eyes widened at the depth of his muscle tone, the sheer size of him, and her hazel eyes turned limpid.

Connor slowly knelt over her, a hand on either side of her head. 'You can still change your mind,' he said softly.

But Mercedes was already shaking her head. 'Are you kidding?' she said, laughing huskily, as she ran her fingertips over the bulging muscles of his upper arms.

Connor grinned. 'Don't tell me, you're a muscles babe at heart.'

Mercedes stopped stroking and looked at him. He was probably teasing her, but the question sounded serious to her. And so she gave it some serious thought. Was she unduly attracted to him because of his size? Because he'd been a soldier? Some of her friends, she knew, were attracted to big men because it gave them some kind of a kick. But one look at his intelligent, warm, just slightly wary eyes, gave her the answer.

She shook her head. 'No, Connor. I'm pretty sure I'd want you even if you were as skinny as a bean pole, and a professor of some obscure branch of algebra.'

Connor laughed. 'Maths was my worst subject at school,' he promised, then the laughter slowly faded from his face to be replaced by a banked, smouldering glow.

Mercedes felt her breath catch at the sheer heat of it. She lifted her head from the pillow, meeting his lips halfway. They were hot and forceful, but led only after asking, and she slipped her tongue between his lips and felt him shudder. She clung to him, pressing against him, feeling heat erupt in every vein, every artery, every sensor on her skin.

The halter top was as a piece of tissue in his hands, and within moments it was lying on the bedroom floor. He cupped her breasts gently, his eyes softening at the sight of her tender pale skin. His thumbs felt a little rough and callused as they flicked across her nipples, and it made her jump on the bed. A hot line of colour flashed across her cheekbones, and suddenly all strength seemed to seep from her. She fell back liquidly against the bed with a soul-deep sigh.

Connor followed her down, his lips swooping onto first one rosebud then the other, tasting and sucking. Then he moved upwards, tracing the line of the delicate bones in her shoulders, moving to her neck, her ears, her throat. She murmured his name restlessly, felt his hands go to the waistband of her shorts, and lifted herself off the bed, helping him undress her. Her naked legs moved sensuously against the denim of his jeans and, with a grunt, he undid his belt, freeing his rapidly hardening body from its painful restriction.

Mercedes slipped her hand between his jeans and briefs, eyes widening at the heat and power she felt there. This time it was Connor's turn to nearly jump off the bed. He laughed. So did she. He bent to kiss her again, long, lingering, a powerfully gentle, yet utterly passionate kiss.

She tugged tellingly on his jeans, then watched as he backed up, stood up, and shed the last of his clothing. Her eyes widened on his naked form, and for a moment – just a moment – a hint of apprehension lit her eyes.

It had been a while.

Then he was above her again, taking his weight on his hands, his knees either side of her hips. Looking down at her, his corn-coloured hair flopped down, and she reached up, brushing back the tendrils of hair, feeling, oddly, suddenly very protective of him.

Slowly, their eyes locked, and he moved onto her. Her legs fell apart, her heels hooking over his calves. Even there he was muscled, and she felt the power of his tendons clench beneath the soles of her feet.

She dug her toes into the flesh of his calves, and massaged.

His eyes got flat and hot.

She reached up to kiss him, her palms spreading luxuriously across his buttocks, pulling him down, at the same time rising up to meet him, knowing that it must be she who made the first, ultimate move. And loving him for it. For all his power and size, Mercedes knew in that instant that she would never be afraid of Connor O'Dell.

She gasped as he entered her, filling every inch, both physically and emotionally. She felt her whole body open up to him, then cried out as he thrust against her, powerful, deep, long and slow. Her fingernails unconsciously began to dig into his back and he made a small animal growl deep in his throat.

Her head thrust back, arching against the pillow, her long black hair becoming hopelessly tangled as she began to thrash her head from side to side.

He kept up the slow, relentless, wonderful pace however, refusing to go faster, even as her frantic cries of encouragement and pleading filled the air. She seemed to float, high above him, for a long, long moment, then slowly sink back. But he was still moving, and the pleasure refused to abate. Once again her cries filled the small, perfumed room, and his back, at some point, began to bleed, tiny red drops of true passion.

Later, much later, Connor's hoarse shout of fulfilment echoed her many others.

Mercedes felt his collapsing weight without tension, instead loving the way he pinioned her to the bed. He lay for a moment in her arms, all his great strength spent. His gasps filled the room, and when he rolled onto his side at last, she reached over and, without leaving the bed, opened the window wider, letting in the warm summer air.

Then she stroked the hair back from his damp face and watched him. She felt as if she could simply do that – watch him – for years and years and years.

Eventually he opened his eyes. 'What?' he said softly.

She smiled and shook her head. 'Nothing,' she said sleepily, happily. 'Nothing at all.' She knew she'd never be able to feel happier than she did at this moment.

It wouldn't ever be possible to feel happier.

That moment when a woman knew she'd finally found the man of her dreams could never be improved upon. Only added to.

* * *

Margaret Wright turned down the tiny alleyway in Oxford's underbelly, and glanced over her shoulder. She wasn't nervous as such, for she knew the score. She'd been around. She was wearing no jewellery, and wore her oldest trouser suit – nothing must stand out, or mark her as a target. She was make-up free, and knew her face looked older than she would normally ever allow it to look, but it was all in a good cause.

All the money she carried on her was the agreed sum – no ID, no credit cards. A friend of a friend had agreed, for a price, to give her the name of her drugs supplier, and although Margaret herself never indulged, knowing drugs to be a fool's game, right at that moment in time she was as eager to get her hands on the stash as any hardened addict.

At the end of the alley was the back door to the small, seedy jazz club, as promised. She didn't knock, but went inside, and stood, as per instructions, in the small entryway. She could smell urine and booze. She wrinkled her nose in distaste then stiffened as one of the doors in front of her opened, revealing, for a moment, a darkened, smoky interior. Even in broad daylight, and hours away from opening time, the miasma of cigarettes, sweat and illegal activity seemed to ooze from the bar and dance floor beyond.

The man who stood watching her looked oddly respectable. A bit like a car salesman. Dressed in a suit and tie, with a good haircut.

'You Busby's friend?' he asked sharply.

Margaret nodded.

'She told you how much?'

Again Margaret nodded and held up the old battered purse she'd found in the back of her wardrobe.

'You wanted E, yeah?'

'No, I don't want E. I thought Busby told you.'

The man, who was younger than Margaret had first thought, grinned, unabashed. 'Oh yeah. Just checking. It pays to be careful.'

Margaret smiled grimly. It did indeed. The sooner she was out of here the better. 'You have the stuff?'

The man patted his top pocket, his brown eyes, previously flat and dismissive, taking on the unmistakable gleam now of greed. 'You got the money?'

Margaret sighed. 'Let me see the stuff.'

'Let me see the money, sweetheart.'

Margaret saw and felt his eyes go over her, obviously unimpressed by what he saw. No doubt he was used to

107

having needy young women fawn over him and Margaret, not used to being found wanting in any man's eyes, even those of a snake like this one, felt her temper rise. Swallowing it back firmly, she opened the purse and withdrew the cash.

'Let's have the stuff,' she said flatly, thrusting the money at him. It occurred to her that if he then refused to hand over the drugs, there was nothing she could do about it. She was alone, and could hardly go whining to the police or the trades description people!

But the man was a professional. Busby, one of his more upper-class customers, was a useful client, and this wasn't the first time she'd sent some of her upper-class friends his way. He handed over the little packet of white powder with unmistakable contempt, however, no doubt wondering how long it would be before she'd be back. Perhaps musing on the chances of getting her into prostitution. Margaret wanted to scream at him that this was not for her, that she was not such a fool, and that she could destroy him like the pipsqueak he was with just a snap of her fingers (and the flexing of her daddy's money), but instead shot him a snarling, savage smile, turned and left.

Fast.

By the time she got back to her car, which she'd parked carefully a long way away, she was feeling dirty and furious. But it was worth it. Inside the car she cast a quick peek at the small plastic envelope of drugs in her pocket and nodded. Perfect. Just perfect.

* * *

Fred Wright looked morosely out of the side window of his chauffeur-driven Rolls-Royce as his driver turned off onto the road to Nether Dene. He couldn't remember the last time he'd visited the village. But the time had come for him and Oriana Foster to have a talk.

'Park on the side of the road near the hotel, Philip, please,' he said, wanting to wait a moment to gather his courage.

From the road, he could see both the Manor House, a small charming cottage with a garden which simply frothed colour, and the entrance to the Dower House Hotel. Fred admired the hotel. Lowell Seton hadn't knocked it about too much, but had instead taken advantage of its classic Georgian beauty to offer his guests a home away from home.

Clever.

Although it was not Lowell Seton that he'd come to see, his cunning choice of parking place made it seem as if his car was just one more of the fleet of Rolls, Bentleys, BMWs and other top-of-the-range cars which the clientele of the hotel preferred.

His rheumy eyes, however, strayed not to the left, and the hotel, but to the right, and the bigger, more ramshackle Manor House, where Oriana Foster now lived. He wasn't, somehow, surprised by her choice of dwelling. But he had to find out what her plans were. He sighed heavily and was reaching for the door handle when a familiar car pulled up on the other, far side of the house, beside an overgrown laurel hedge.

His hand stilled on the chrome handle as he watched his daughter get out of the low-slung scarlet sports car and look around.

His Rolls was not particularly distinctive as far as they went, and he knew she wouldn't be able to read the number plate from where she was. He also doubted if Margaret even gave a thought as to what he did with his days, or what his private life might contain.

As he'd expected, she didn't even give his car a second glance. She did, however, look around in a very long, careful way, and something about her – perhaps the tense, gleeful way she walked – made the hairs stand up on the back of his neck.

Fred knew his only child well: her wilfulness, her ruthlessness, her greed. He was already scared about where her obsession with Lowell Seton was going to lead them. Now he felt downright terrified. When she disappeared into the grounds, he got out and walked slowly up the road, looking every minute of his age. His driver watched him go, a puzzled look on his face. Reluctance was obvious in every step his employer took, and he wondered who the old man was visiting. It certainly wasn't a place the driver had ever been to before, and he'd been driving for the Supermarket King for nearly ten years now.

He watched the old man disappear into the driveway and shrugged. He knew when something wasn't his business. He'd have been positively astonished (and even more sure than ever that it was none of his business) if he'd been able to see what Fred Wright, multi-millionaire, did next. He stepped off the path, avoiding the front door altogether, and tiptoed, actually tiptoed, into the nearest stand of bushes. From there he gradually and cautiously circumnavigated the house.

He saw his daughter the moment he turned the corner on the east-facing wall; she was staring in the open kitchen window. Then she glanced once behind her, before, as agilely as any athlete, her petite figure only helping and abetting her, she slithered inside.

Fred leaned heavily against the trunk of the big cedar tree under which he was hiding. He had no idea what Margaret was doing. He only knew it wasn't good. He turned and left the way he came, walking back to the car like a bitter, defeated, hopeless old man. Back in the rear seat, he sighed heavily. Catching the driver's eyes in the rear-view mirror, his face hardened.

'Back to Penny Farthing, Philip,' he said.

He suddenly needed to be home, where things were familiar, and at least gave the *impression* of being safe. As the car pulled silently away, picked up speed past the deserted grounds of the Manor and pulled away from Nether Dene, Fred Wright nodded to himself in the back.

He'd done right, going to his solicitors last week and getting his will changed. He would ring them up when he got back and ask them if it was ready for signing. The sooner he got it down in black and white the better it would be.

Inside the Manor House kitchen, Margaret Wright carefully hid the stash of Class A drugs and left by the same open window as she'd arrived.

Three rooms away, in the sitting room, Oriana was on the telephone, listening to the apologetic voice of Marcus Royle. So Lowell knew, she thought drearily. More trouble. At some point she thought she heard a scraping noise in the kitchen, but put it down to the attention of a stray cat which she'd begun feeding, and didn't bother to go and investigate. She had more important things to worry about. Or so she thought.

NINE

Mercedes stretched luxuriantly, then yawned. Sitting up, she glanced down beside her to see Connor gazing up at her, similarly sleepy and equally loath to move.

'Come on, up and at 'em,' she said encouragingly. 'We can't stay in bed all afternoon.'

'Why not?'

'Dogs to feed. Walks to be taken. Dinner to cook. We never *did* get around to that spaghetti, remember?' Connor grumbled but got up, padding huge and naked onto the landing. She could hear him opening doors until he found the bathroom, and a moment later, the running of the shower.

She grinned, got out of bed and reached for a pink satin wrap. Slipping it over her bare shoulders she walked to the bathroom and peeked inside. One look told her that Connor did indeed take up the whole shower cubicle. So, either she'd have to get a bigger shower installed, or she'd have to lose weight – drastically. There was no other way they were *both* going to fit in there!

She made her way to the kitchen, put on the kettle, and collected the afternoon mail – an RSVP from one of her old friends, saying she'd be glad to come to her birthday party. She asked if she could bring along her ex as a partner, her current amour having swanned off to the South of France with a television production assistant.

Mercedes grimaced in sympathy and amusement, then made a little sound and headed for the phone. This reminded her. She tapped out Margaret's mobile.

'Hello?'

'Hello, it's me, Mercedes. I forgot to call you about my dress for the weekend.'

There was a long pause. 'Huh?' Margaret Wright said vaguely.

Mercedes laughed. 'Sorry, you wanted to know what colour I was going to wear at my birthday party?'

'Oh, yeah, right.'

'You know, so we wouldn't clash?' Mercedes went on, smiling, thinking that only a social butterfly like Margaret would even care about something like that. 'Well, it's gold.'

'Oh, OK.'

'Margaret, are you all right?' she asked curiously. Something about the older woman sounded slightly off. She'd spoken to her brother's girlfriend on the phone many times, and she'd always been brimming over with confidence and verve. It wasn't like her to be so distracted.

'Yeah, fine. Gold, right. OK, I'll probably show up in red. Looking forward to it,' Margaret said abruptly.

Mercedes, sensing that the other woman was about to hang up – again, an unusual sign, for Margaret could chat on the phone all day – added quickly, 'Oh, by the way, I'd better warn you. Oriana Foster will probably be there.'

This time there was no mistaking the quality of the silence on the other end of the line. She thought she heard a swiftly indrawn breath too, but when Margaret spoke, it was with a wary caution which was, once more, an uncharacteristic sign. 'Oh? You think that's wise? Won't Lowell be upset?'

'Oh, he already knows. You know, Margaret, we're beginning to think, both of us, that we've got it wrong. About Oriana and Rollo, I mean. Oriana's even asked me for help in finding out what really happened to Rollo.'

113

'But surely we know?' Margaret's voice snapped across the line.

Mercedes sighed. 'Perhaps. But I've been giving it some more thought, and I remembered how Rollo was that last summer, all excited about some sort of family project or other. I'm helping Oriana to find out what it was all about. Wouldn't it be great if it turned out Oriana was innocent after all? I know Lowell would be so relieved . . .' Mercedes trailed off abruptly, suddenly realizing that she was being less than tactful. 'Anyway,' she concluded hastily, 'I just thought I'd let you know about the party.' And, hearing movement upstairs, tacked on hastily, 'See ya!' and hung up.

She walked to the foot of the stairs and smiled. 'You better not have used up all the hot water!' she threatened playfully.

* * *

Lowell didn't pause to knock, but pushed open the slightly warped front door and walked into the hall. 'Hello,' he called loudly, and heard movement off to his right. A moment later the door to the main living room opened and Oriana looked out.

She was dressed in a crisp white dress, and her feet were bare. Her curly hair was pulled back under a white bandanna, which she quickly whipped off as she saw Lowell. It left her golden curls hopelessly mussed. Big, sombre blue eyes regarded him warily.

'Lowell,' she greeted him nervously.

Lowell smiled grimly. 'Oriana. You keep managing to surprise me. Care to tell me how come you're the real new owner of this place?' he asked tightly, indicating the old house all around him. It was only then that he suddenly realized that the letter he'd written to OxonCountryProp asking them to fire her had probably come back to her for assessment, and he felt his blood heat as he imagined how she must have laughed herself sick over that little incident.

She sighed. 'You'd better come in,' she said bleakly.

He followed her into the room, shaking his head as she indicated a seat. 'I think I have a right to know, don't you?' he demanded.

'No, I don't,' Oriana said quietly. She sat herself down gracefully onto the sofa and looked up at his dumbfounded face with real regret. Why was it they could never meet without arguing? Without her having to hurt him – yet again?

'If I'd really killed your brother, then yes, I'd owe you big time,' she explained patiently. 'But I didn't touch him, Lowell. That means I don't owe you a thing.'

Lowell's grey eyes narrowed. 'You have a very good way of avoiding answering awkward questions,' he said grimly. 'Shock tactics. Beats good old prevarication any day.'

Oriana sighed again. 'Lowell, it wouldn't do you any good to know how I came to buy the Manor. If I told you that I don't really know how, you wouldn't believe me anyway, would you?'

'Too right I wouldn't,' he snapped. What did she take him for?

Oriana shrugged her slender shoulders. 'There you go then,' she said. In truth, she didn't actually *know* the name of her benefactor. So what she'd said was true. The fact that she could take a good guess was neither here nor there.

Lowell shook his head. 'You really do take the gold medal for gall, you know that, don't you?' he said. 'Just tell me this: did Rollo have anything to do with it? With you coming into money, I mean?'

Oriana looked so genuinely astonished that he couldn't help but believe her when she shook her head violently. 'No! Hell, no. How could he have?' she demanded. 'Rollo didn't have any money, not any real money. Did he?' she added curiously, after a moment's thought.

Lowell shook his head. 'No. No, he didn't. I just needed to hear you say it, that's all.' He moved from the fireplace, where he'd been leaning against the mantelpiece, and walked slowly towards the window, hands thrust moodily into his pockets. His brother hadn't even had a paying job when he died. And the family had still been struggling to come up with the inheritance tax after their father's death.

'As far as I know, the only time Rollo ever talked about money was when he was joking,' he confirmed sadly. 'Like when he joked that the painting hanging up in Mercedes' room was really worth a fortune.' He turned and looked at Oriana, a wry grimace on his face. 'It was an undistinguished oil painting by an amateur painter who'd lived in the village at the beginning of the last century. Mercedes bought it for a fiver from the local village fête. Took up all her pocket money. That about sums up the state of our finances after Dad died.'

Oriana nodded, actually remembering the village fête when Mercedes had bought the painting. Her friend, only fifteen at the time, had liked it because it was a village scene which she could actually recognize.

Oriana smiled back. 'I remember her buying it,' she said thoughtfully. 'We said it was only donated to the sale because its owner didn't want to give it wall room any longer.'

Lowell smiled, infinitesimally relaxing. 'But she loved it,' he added, his voice warm with fond remembrance. 'She took it with her when she moved into the cottage. I think it's still hanging in her bedroom now.'

Oriana nodded, her eyes soft and cornflower blue. For the first time, he realized, she actually looked relaxed in his presence. Her usual tense, wary, hard edge was nowhere to be seen. And he realized, in that moment, that he too felt different. Where was the hopeless rage he felt whenever she was near? The helpless desire. The vague, unnamed emotion which kept him awake at night, or tormented his dreams whenever he did manage to doze?

'Oriana,' he said softly, 'did you kill Rollo?'

She looked at him. 'No.'

She made no attempt to persuade him. Gave no pleas or arguments to back up her flat denial. But the single, powerful syllable was enough to send the last of his defences crashing down. He took a step towards her, and saw hope flare in her eyes as she saw that there was something new in his face. She rose from the sofa, one hand half held out, as if not daring to believe what she was seeing in his eyes. Her hand faltered and fell back to her side.

Lowell took another step towards her. 'If I said I believed you, would it make a difference?' he asked, swallowing painfully against the lump in his throat. The roaring sound of his own laboured heartbeat in his ears threatened to drown out her answer, but he could already see it in her eyes anyway. Those big, lovely blue eyes.

'Of course it would,' Oriana all but whispered. 'It would mean the difference between life and mere existence,' she added, wondering if she would ever be able to explain to him what her life had been like in prison, all those years: the frustration of being believed to be guilty, when she knew she was innocent; the fear of those first few months, as she wondered about drug addiction, sexual assault, or getting on the wrong side of the 'top dog'; of the sheer dreariness of the years which followed. The battle against becoming institutionalized, making friends, only to see them leave years before you knew you'd get out yourself, and trying not to feel jealous, but happy for them instead.

And all the time, the only thing that had kept her going had been the thought of one day getting out: of seeing Lowell; of talking to Lowell; of breathing the same air as Lowell; of proving her innocence to Lowell; of seeing just that look on his face which she'd seen moments before; of knowing that she had, at long last, a chance with Lowell.

But how could she put anything so profound into words?

'The difference between life and existing,' Lowell slowly repeated her words. And nodded. Yes, how well that explained it. Before, when Oriana had been in prison, he'd merely been existing. He'd saved the family from bankruptcy, built up a first-class hotel, diversified, and put himself well on the way to being a millionaire twice over.

But it had given him no joy, no sense of achievement, no pleasure at all. He only started to live, as opposed to merely exist, the day he'd looked up and seen Oriana, standing there in the garden in front of him. He'd felt hate. Or thought it was hate. He'd felt rage, and need. Oh yes, he'd come alive again all right. But now he was feeling none of those things, but something else totally different. Something which was struggling to rise to the surface, like the tender but ferociously determined green shoots of a plant coming through concrete.

Love.

He wasn't aware of moving those last few steps, but suddenly he was right beside her. Her eyes were glowing. With love as well? He'd always known that he'd loved her, but was it possible that she loved him too? That their mutual teenage attraction had blossomed, after all that it had going against it, into a thriving, green thing?

'Don't play games with me, Oriana,' he said thickly. 'Not now. I can't take it right now. I believe you when you say you didn't kill Rollo. Now tell me . . .'

But he couldn't say it. What if he was wrong? If he'd misread the signs? What if she just saw him as another victim, someone who deserved to have his pain eased, but nothing more? What if all she wanted from him was his admission that he no longer thought her guilty of murder? Nothing more?

What would he do then, with all the years that amounted to the rest of his life? Could he really live them without Oriana? After thirteen years without her, could he manage another thirteen? And another thirteen after that, and after that, until all the years were used up?

'What? Lowell, what?' Oriana cried. 'Just ask me!'

'Do you love me?' he all but snarled.

Oriana laughed, a mixture of sheer joy, disbelief that this moment could be happening at all, and the release of years of almost unbearable tension. Then she saw him flinch, and abruptly the semi-hysterical laughter was cut off.

'Oh, Lowell, of course I love you,' she said humbly. 'Surely you know that?'

* * *

118

Margaret Wright stared at her mobile phone for a long, long time, Mercedes' words echoing around in her head. What was it with the Seton family? Were they all moon-struck by that damned whey-faced witch? What kind of spell could Oriana Foster cast which could bewitch both brother and sister? And what had Mercedes meant when she said that Lowell would be relieved if Oriana were proved to be innocent?

But, of course, she knew. Deep down, she already knew. She rammed the phone into her bag and got out of the car, fury in every line of her rigid figure. She'd been on her way back from Nether Dene when Mercedes' cheerful chatter about dress colours had interrupted her gleeful contemplation of what she'd just done. Now all the pleasure in getting rid of her rival seemed to drizzle out of her. She tossed her platinum blonde head angrily and walked briskly to the main doors of Penny Farthing, the huge sprawling house which had been her home ever since her father had struck it big with his first supermarket.

As she entered the hall, built in almost baronial proportions, she saw, through one of the open doors, her father sitting in his study, nodding off over his paper. He really was getting old, she mused. But Lowell would make a fine new chairman. As son-in-law to the old man, and with his proven track record as a businessman, she was sure she could get him on the board. She already had enough stocks and shares to wield considerable power.

Ignoring her father's dozing form, she walked into the study next door and reached for the phone. Now to tip off the police. She'd just put her fingertips to the receiver when she hesitated. Were telephone calls to the police recorded nowadays? She wasn't sure. But she certainly didn't want to have her voice recorded somewhere. The tip-off which would put Oriana Foster back behind bars, where she belonged, had to be anonymous.

Completely anonymous.

She already knew, in her heart of hearts, that she was only hanging on to Lowell by the skin of her fingertips. If he ever found out that she was the one behind that witch's return to prison, he might just use it as an excuse to end things between them.

Slowly, she wandered over to the writing desk, pulled out a pair of scissors, a plain sheet of paper and some glue. Then she went into the study to steal her father's newspaper. As she lifted it off his sleeping lap and turned back to walk towards the open door, she had no idea that Fred Wright's eyes had opened and were following her exit thoughtfully. Sadly. And with a knowing resignation which would surely have given her pause for thought, had she seen it.

* * *

Oriana slowly lowered her lips to his shoulder, tasting the faint tang of salt on her tongue. It was another hot day outside and, as she licked the sweat from his skin, she felt him shudder.

They were lying on the carpet in front of the big fireplace, which was dark and unlit on such a warm summer's day. She wasn't quite sure how they'd got there – had she pulled him down, or had he lowered her? But what did it matter? He was lying beneath her, and her hands were inside his shirt after she'd feverishly undone his buttons, ripping off one in her haste and need. That was all that mattered.

Now she slowly lowered her tongue, following the line of his throat down and across his chest, before sucking gently on the button of flesh she found there. His chest was hairless and deeply tanned, and she felt the gooseflesh rise up against his ribcage as she teased him with tiny scratches of her fingernails.

When she lifted her head to look at him, a high flush spread across his taut cheekbones, and his grey eyes were the colour of thunderclouds, heavy with rain.

She felt his hands on the back of her dress, heard and felt the zip being lowered, and the warm air dancing along her suddenly naked spine. Then the four hot points of his fingers took over, along with the caressing rub of his thumb, turning in slow, lazy circles in the small of her back.

Her knees turned instantly to jelly. She still couldn't believe that this was all happening. Any of it. That he believed, truly *believed*, that she was innocent. That he *loved* her. Wanted her. Needed her. And was making love to her.

It all seemed too much to be true, somehow. Never in her life had she had such luck, been given so much of everything. It was as if someone had handed her her heart's desire on a silver platter, and she felt, with a superstitious shudder of dread, a sense of foreboding. As if somewhere, something must surely be lurking, waiting to take it all away from her again. As if fate, after having been so cruel to her, could hardly be expected to change its habit now.

Then Lowell reached up and kissed her, his hands urgent in her curls, his mouth hot and needy, and she moaned his name and kissed him back, her fear fleeing in the face of his passion.

* * *

In the little reading room off the main library, Margaret Wright began to cut out words and letters from the newspaper. In his study, Fred Wright reached for the telephone and dialled a number. His hand was shaking.

* * *

Lowell inhaled sharply as her tongue darted into his navel, like a burrowing missile, making him arch off the floor and throw his head back helplessly. 'Oriana,' he moaned.

She reached for his belt and, as she slipped it free, the telephone rang. They hardly heard it.

She pulled the belt through, then snapped open the buttons. He half sat up, pulling the dress over her head and staring speechlessly at her pale, supple body. Then he leaned forward and kissed first one rose-coloured nipple, then the other. Oriana gasped, her eyes closing, a rapt expression on her face. She cradled his head tenderly, biting her lip as she felt the heat expand and take control of her body.

The phone continued its plaintive tolling.

She reached down to kiss his shoulder again, then, when she felt his hands on her panties, lifted her knees from the floor to enable him to undress her. Her own hands went to work, feverishly stripping him too. He was beautiful. Just as she'd always known he would be beautiful. As she gazed down at him, the telephone stopped ringing. She was barely aware that it had ever started.

All fear had left her now. This was how it was always meant to be, and nothing could stop it, or take it away from her. Lowell loved her. Lowell was naked beneath her, his face tight with desire, his eyes smoky with passion. Nothing that life could do to her could hurt her now.

She reached down and lowered herself on to him, tensing just a little as she felt her body being entered for the first time. She gave a gasp and a tiny wince as the final barrier was broken, and she saw his eyes snap open.

'Oriana,' he croaked, half in question, but then she clenched her knees on either side of his hips with a tight, possessive power, her own inner muscles similarly clenching tight around him, making him repeat her name, but this time almost as a scream.

'Oriana!'

* * *

Margaret Wright slid the slightly sticky piece of paper into an envelope. She licked it down, then regarded the bare white square. Should she put some sort of address on it? She shrugged. Hell no, it wasn't as if she was going to post it. She wanted action now. Before it was too late.

She put the envelope with its poisonous little message into her bag and grabbed her car keys.

* * *

From his chair by the window, Fred watched his only child walk to her sports car and roar off down the road. He had a dull ache in his chest which felt far too physical for his liking, and he tried to ease it by rubbing it with a palsied hand. He was used to Margaret making his heart ache, but this was something more. Still, at least his new will was signed, so if the worse came to the worst . . .

He stared at the phone, wondering just how long he could afford to wait before trying to reach Oriana Foster again. How much time did they both have? As the sound of his daughter's sports car faded in the distance, he thought grimly that it probably wasn't long.

Not long at all.

* * *

Oriana moaned, her head falling forward as yet again the tidal wave of pleasure swept over her. Lowell caught her collapsing figure in his arms and deftly turned her, rolling over her and watching her face as he lunged into her.

She opened her eyes to look up at him, loving the way his sweat-damp raven hair clung to his brow, the dark desire still rampant in his eyes. She rose to meet him, lunge for lunge, moan for moan, her breasts brushing against the hardness of his chest as he lowered his head to bury his face in her neck and breathe in the scent of her.

His powerful loins tensed, then melted, and his head shot back as he gave a low, final, shuddering moan. Oriana grabbed his face between her hands. 'Look at me!' she commanded, and he did so, his face naked and vulnerable, yet completely triumphant, and she knew that he must see his own expression mirrored on her own face.

With fierce exultation, she clung to him, holding him close, as the sweat cooled on their bodies and again, unanswered, the telephone pealed away in the next room.

* * *

Margaret Wright pulled into the car park at Bicester Crown Court, not wanting to park in the actual police station next door. She got out, crossed the side road separating the two buildings, and looked around cautiously. She peered inside before entering, glad that she did so, as she saw at once the desk sergeant manning his post.

Damn! How was she going to leave the letter without being seen?

She walked around the side of the building, but her way was quickly barred. She almost growled in frustration. She could hardly hang around here all day, pacing around and attracting attention, but she was not going to leave before getting rid of the letter. She didn't really want to have to bribe some kid to take it in for her.

Then she stopped as a furious swearing and cursing seemed to start up right beside her. She jumped, then cautiously looked around to the front of the building once more.

A young constable was escorting a very unkempt and extremely drunk middle-aged man up the steps.

Waiting a few brief moments, Margaret took a deep breath then followed them inside. She'd always had the courage to take risks. Probably because she'd always thought that life's little rules didn't apply to her. And, once again, her faith in her own arrogance proved justified as she saw the desk was now temporarily empty. Towards the back of the building, she could hear rumbling, calming voices, overlaid by foul-mouthed threats. Darting to the desk, she placed the envelope where the sergeant could hardly miss it, then slipped outside.

When she got behind the wheel, she was smiling. The Cheshire cat, in that moment, would have had nothing on Margaret Wright.

* * *

Oriana didn't want him to go, but she could tell he needed time alone. As she watched him dress, her eyes somnolent but with the possessiveness of a new lover, Oriana sighed blissfully.

Lowell glanced at her, smiled uncertainly, and tucked his shirt into his trousers.

Her virginity had shaken him. Then her passion had overwhelmed him, in a way which he knew he would want to experience again and again. But he had to think. And he couldn't think with her looking at him like that. He glanced down at her. 'I'll be back,' he said softly.

She smiled. 'I know,' she said devastatingly.

Then he was gone.

For a long while she lay there, naked and appeased, and then the phone rang. Again. She frowned, vaguely remembering that its annoying buzz had been ringing on and off throughout the afternoon. With a sigh, supposing it must be important for whoever it was to keep on trying, she slid back into her dress and walked through to the small study.

She lifted the receiver. 'Yes?'

'Oriana Foster?'

The voice was male, and one she didn't recognize. She felt herself stiffen.

'Yes,' she repeated warily.

'You're in trouble,' the voice said promptly. It sounded old and tired but not dramatic. Nor even, oddly enough, considering what it was saying, threatening. 'Margaret Wright was in your house earlier today, without your knowledge. She must have had some reason. Be careful.'

'But what . . . Hello?' Oriana, with only the dial tone sounding in her ear, stared at the telephone receiver blankly. Then all her earlier fear came rushing back with a vengeance.

It *had* been too good to last, after all.

TEN

Oriana staggered to the sink and held on tightly to its cold porcelain edges, providing her with meagre comfort as dry heaves shook her slender frame. After all these years, for that old familiar fear to be back was almost more than she could bear.

At the trial, she'd known things were going badly for her, especially after Frances Greer's perjured testimony. Fear had been her constant companion; cold, hard, and seemingly indestructible. She'd tried to tell herself that innocent people weren't convicted, but she already suspected that that was not true.

All during the days of her trial, she had suffered the skin-crawling sensation of avid eyes staring down at her from the public gallery, the coolly impersonal animosity of the prosecuting counsel only adding to the weight bearing down on her. She'd also felt guilty about the bewildered presence of her aunt, who loved her, but had been hopelessly out of her depth. At night, she snatched portions of sleep, but always woke to a feeling of dread deep in the pit of her stomach, the same cold dread which was in her stomach now.

Oriana slammed her clenched hands down on the old-fashioned sink and shook her head. 'No, no, no, no,' she gasped, over and over again. She wouldn't let that old feeling of helpless terror defeat her once again.

After she had stood in frozen numbness in the dock as the 'guilty' verdict was handed down, she thought she'd seen the end of it, forever. Because the worst had at last happened. After that, what was there left to be afraid of? And, during the years in prison, it had never come back.

But now she was free, and knew that her freedom could be taken away again. Even now, she could feel it draining from her.

What had Margaret Wright *done*?

She slowly straightened up from the sink, her dry heaves abating as she forced herself to take control. She needed to think. She had been in all day, mostly in the den or the living room, so Margaret hadn't been in there. She would surely not have gone in through the front door for fear of being seen. The back then. Most of those rooms were deserted, still empty and bare for the moment, with no hiding places.

It had to be the kitchen.

Oriana looked slowly around her, the hairs standing up on the nape of her neck, as if expecting a dragon to come rearing out of a food cupboard, bellowing fire. But only blank-looking units and rather tired floorboards stared back at her mundanely.

She realized with a sinking heart that she didn't have a clue where to start. Or even what she was looking for.

Oriana shook her head. *Think, dammit. Think!* One thing was for certain: she needed help.

Her first thought was to go after Lowell, but even as she yearned to do just that, a colder, harder part of her psyche was vetoing it. She'd only just got Lowell back. And he'd only just begun to trust her again. If she went to him now with some wild tale about anonymous telephone calls, and Margaret Wright being in her house . . .

Margaret, his girlfriend.

Oriana moaned and shook her head, wrapping her arms around her waist, rocking backwards and forwards as misery swamped her. Would the nightmare ever end?

How could she persuade Lowell to give Margaret up without telling him about her suspicions — and without proof? But now that they were lovers, how could she ever share him? And with *Margaret*, of all people?

It was the ticking of the ponderous 1950s clock on the wall which finally snapped her attention back from the brink of the abyss. Time was wasting. And she was sure that whatever it was that Margaret had done, she wasn't wasting *her* time right now. But who could she turn to for help? Who was there who would believe in her, and, even more to the point, know what to do next?

Suddenly Oriana gave a little yelp, called herself all kinds of a fool, and sprinted for the door. She should never have given Connor the afternoon off.

* * *

Mercedes stepped out of the shower and donned a clean pair of white shorts and a skimpy lime-green T-shirt. She was still rubbing her damp raven hair when she walked into the kitchen and found Connor clearing away the cold lunch things.

'Tea?' he asked, looking at her out of lazy green eyes, wondering why women ever bothered to wear make-up or have fancy haircuts when they looked so good natural, all damp and rosy from a shower. Or was it only Mercedes who could look so beautiful, whatever the circumstance?

'Lovely,' Mercedes nodded. 'Milk, no sugar.'

Connor had just put the kettle on, when the kitchen door flew open. Oriana catapulted inside, then came to a quick stop. It would have been almost comical, if she hadn't looked so worried. She looked first at Mercedes, obviously fresh from a shower, and glowing as a woman only can when she's just made love. She wondered, briefly, if she had the same look about her. Or had her terror since wiped it away? Then she looked at Connor.

She'd known where to find him, of course. She was not blind, and had been well aware of the romance blossoming between her friend and her bodyguard. And she approved. Connor was a good man, a strong and decent one, and she couldn't have wished for a better mate for her friend. But right now she needed him more.

One look at Oriana's pale face, her eyes bright with uncharacteristic fear, was enough for Connor. He put down the kettle slowly.

'Trouble?'

Oriana, unable to speak, nodded mutely.

Connor went straight to Mercedes, kissed her on the forehead, and said softly, 'I'll call you later.'

Mercedes opened her mouth to protest, then abruptly closed it again. Perhaps it was the look in his green eyes which warned her. Or perhaps she sensed herself the extreme plight of the other woman. Whatever it was, it was enough to silence her.

But as she watched them go, she couldn't help but feel a certain sense of resentment. After all, Connor had just left her bed, literally, to jump to the beck and call of another woman. And Oriana, to be more precise, someone whom Mercedes still couldn't fathom.

She had a right to be hurt, didn't she?

Oriana was walking so fast back to the Manor she was almost running. Not that that worried Connor, whose long legs were easily able to keep up with her, and, indeed, make him look as if he was merely strolling at that.

Inside the big house, Oriana went straight to the kitchen. She was shaking.

Connor closed the door behind him and leaned against it. 'Easy,' he said softly. He'd never seen Oriana look so fragile before. Or so unsure of herself.

Oriana nodded, took a long slow breath, and let it out.

'Someone was in here earlier,' she said, and saw him flush.

Connor bit back a curse only with difficulty. A sharp sense of guilt sent the blood rushing from his face. He should have been here. Dammit, he was her *bodyguard*! He should never have agreed to take the afternoon off, but with nothing happening on the job, he'd allowed himself to be lulled into a false sense of security.

'Are you all right?' he asked gruffly.

'Yes, I'm fine,' Oriana said dismissively. It was not her personal safety she was worried about. Well, not her *physical* safety, anyway. The thought of going back to prison still scared her almost beyond rational thought.

'Did you see who it was?' Connor asked sharply.

'Yes. No. That is, I know who it was,' Oriana said, somewhat impatiently, but she wasn't about to go into the whole anonymous telephone call thing right now. She waved a hand in the air, indicating that she needed him to be quiet for a moment. To give her space to think.

Connor immediately snapped his mouth closed.

Oriana forced the panic away, and began to work things out logically. All right. What would Margaret Wright want? Well, if she suspected what was going on between her and Lowell, she'd want her, Oriana, out of the way. Right. But she hadn't confronted Oriana. Hadn't threatened her. Hadn't hired someone to 'persuade' her to leave the village. After her time in prison, Oriana had no doubts about the harsh realities of life. If someone as rich as Margaret Wright wanted her out of the way, she'd be got out of the way. But the other woman hadn't gone down that route. Instead, she'd sneaked into the house, probably whilst Oriana was still in the living room. That was taking a huge risk.

Why?

Oriana slowly raised her head and fixed Connor with a grim, hard stare. He preferred it to her earlier panic. *Much* preferred it.

'Connor,' she said quietly, 'if you wanted to get someone out of the way, someone who was on parole from prison, what would you do?'

Connor stared at her for a moment, instantly following her line of thought. His face became as grim as her own. 'That's easy,' he said gruffly. 'I'd get the terms of that person's parole broken. And seen to be broken. Then it's back to the pokey.'

Oriana nodded. 'All right. What's the easiest way of doing that?'

'Proving they'd committed a felony,' he said promptly. 'Or proving they'd been consorting with known felons.'

'Okay, forget the latter. Stick to the proof-of-crime theory. What would you do if you wanted to prove that someone had committed a serious offence, but needed to do the dirty work yourself as opposed to hiring thugs, and yet only had limited physical resources.'

Connor squinted his eyes in thought for a while, then nodded. 'Easy. I'd plant drugs on the person's property, then tip off the police.'

Oriana looked around the kitchen helplessly. Drugs could be hidden in such a tiny packet. And it would only take one E pill to get her sent back to prison.

'We're never going to be able to search the place in time,' she heard herself say, as if from a long way off. Already the police could be on their way. And what if it wasn't in the kitchen after all? She felt herself sway, and clung on to the sink grimly. The fear was back. Like a vulture, circling in the sky, giving a triumphant cry as it spotted carrion.

She was going to go back to prison. Again. It wasn't fair. She couldn't do it. Not again.

She felt movement, then a moment later, something hard against the back of her legs. She felt herself pitching forward and cried out, but it was only Connor, forcing her head down between her knees. He'd propelled her on to a chair and was saying something to her. His voice was hard, forceful, pushing past the despair.

'Oriana, listen. Take deep breaths. Stay calm. I've got an idea. All right?'

She managed to grab a few deep breaths and felt the cold shaking subside a little. She felt only numb now. Blissfully numb. And she knew that feeling, too.

The worst had happened. Again. Ah well, it was better than fear.

She slowly straightened up, having no idea of the bleakness in her eyes, or the total absence of colour in her face.

Connor swore silently to himself, wanting to find whoever had done this to her and rip him to shreds. Instead, he took her cold hands in his and leaned forward on his haunches. 'Oriana, listen. I have an old friend, an ex-copper— No, wait,' he said, as she made to withdraw her hands and made a brief mewing sound at the mention of the word 'copper'. 'Like I said, he's not in the force anymore. He works for me, in fact, as a night watchman. Better pay, easier hours,' he grinned, forcing himself to talk calmly, normally, to keep her anchored back in the real world.

She couldn't go spacey on him. Not now.

'The thing is, he used to be in the drug squad, as a canine handler. Those dogs have a fairly short working life, and are usually retired and farmed out after the police no longer need them, to private security firms, private homes, what have you. But when Pete left, he was allowed to take the dog with him. He uses him on night patrol now, although he's not technically a guard dog. But the villains don't know that. He only lives a few miles away. If I ask him, as a favour and with no questions asked, he'll bring Garbo the pooch over, and believe me, that Labrador will have found anything there is to be found before you can say Jack Robinson. Yeah?'

Oriana blinked, and he was relieved to see some of the shock fading from her eyes.

'A sniffer dog?' she said uncertainly.

Connor nodded. Good. She was listening to him. Functioning. He took out his phone and made the call.

Oriana waited. And waited.

Connor glanced at her. 'He'll be asleep. Like I said, he's a night watchman. We've got to give him time to ge— Hey, Pete? It's me. The big cheese. Look I need a favour. I need you and Garbo to come to this address straight away. Manor House, Nether Dene. You know it? Good. No, I can't say

132

over the phone. But it's priority one, OK? Get here as fast as you can. Oh, and, Pete, when you get here, if there are cop cars all over the place, turn around and go home, and you never heard from me. All right?'

Connor listened, then nodded, then hung up.

'Right. Let's get started in here. You never know,' Connor said, pulling Oriana to her feet, knowing she needed to get busy, otherwise waiting for Pete and the dog to turn up would drive her crazy. 'We might get lucky.'

Oriana nodded, but looked around listlessly. Where to start?

'Let's start with the food cupboards. Check any opened packets. Especially the cereal and dried food stuffs, like lentils or semolina. Oriana, get cracking,' he finished sharply.

'Right,' she said dully.

Connor began grimly and systematically checking the U-bend under the sink and the pipework which was easily accessible. If Oriana had told him that she knew it was a woman, he probably wouldn't have bothered with the plumbing. But it was a favourite stashing place with men, so that's where he went first.

* * *

Margaret Wright dialled Mercedes' number and paced her bedroom, waiting for it to be answered. A genuine Turner hung on the wall, and in her acres of closet space hung outfits from Paris, Milan and Rome. In the vault, hidden behind a Venetian mirror, were diamonds and rubies, emeralds, pearls and sapphires. She could have got into one of four top-of-the-range cars and driven to the airport to board an aeroplane to any destination she chose. The Caribbean. Monte Carlo. The Seychelles. But right now she felt as if her whole life was held in the balance, captive to a little nobody who should never have resurfaced in the first place.

What the hell was she, Margaret Wright, doing, hanging on the phone, her nerves screaming, desperate for information? That was for losers. And she was no loser. Never had been, never would be.

'Hello? Connor? Why—'

'Mercedes, it's me. Sorry not to be Connor by the way. Who is he? He sounds dishy.' She forced her voice to be its usual gay, gossipy self. But her knuckles, as they clutched the phone, were white with tension.

'Connor? Oh, he's . . . well, you've met him. Big, blond, gorgeous.' Mercedes' voice, on the end of the line, sounded distinctly cagey.

Sensing trouble, Margaret abruptly stopped pacing. Big and blond? 'You're not talking about Oriana Foster's live-in lover, are you?' she asked, genuinely scandalized. What the hell was happening over there? First Lowell going out of his mind, and now Mercedes.

Mercedes laughed, a shade shame-facedly. 'Yes, the same. Although they're not lovers. We are,' she said firmly. 'He'll be at the party, too,' she added, her tone of voice just daring Margaret to make something of it.

But Margaret was too smart for that. Besides, she had other things to worry about.

'Oh, right. OK, thanks for letting me know. The reason I called is I was thinking about what you said earlier. You know, about Rollo and what really happened that summer. If' – and here she had to grit her teeth and force the sweetness out through a mental wringer – 'as you and Lowell now seem to think, Oriana didn't do it, I was wondering if I could help you find out who did. You know, come up with ideas and thoughts. I was wondering what progress you'd made.'

So saying, she found herself literally holding her breath.

Mercedes, who was dishing out dog food in her kitchen, the phone tucked under her chin and hunched against her shoulder, paused, fork in mid-air. Margaret, offering to help? That was new. Then her frown disappeared. 'Oh yes, I forgot. You were there that summer, weren't you. Just back from . . . where was it? Switzerland?' No wonder Margaret was curious. She'd been hovering on the fringes, so to speak.

134

'Austria,' Margaret corrected automatically. 'I'd had to butter up Cousin Veronica, who was going out there with her parents.'

Mercedes nodded. Right, she remembered now. Margaret's father, Fred, had been in the process of building his first supermarket by then, in Banbury, and hadn't yet hit it big time in the money stakes.

'Well, there's not much been happening yet,' Mercedes said, thinking about Oriana bursting in on them, whey-faced and panicky.

But she was not about to go into that with Margaret. Not only did she still feel loyalty towards Oriana, she somehow knew that Margaret would find out about Connor being there with her, and then dumping her the moment Oriana crooked her little finger, and she was still smarting about it, and certainly in no mood to hear Margaret's commiserations.

'Oh. Well, I was just wondering,' Margaret said, sounding, oddly enough, relieved.

'I did have one idea though,' Mercedes added, just as the older woman was on the verge of making her excuses and hanging up. 'I remembered Rollo kept a diary. A big old thing, leather-bound, with an old-fashioned lock on it. I wondered if he'd written anything useful in it — perhaps what he'd been doing that last summer.'

Margaret Wright froze. 'Oh?' she mumbled.

'Hmm. Thing is, I'm not sure where the diary is,' Mercedes mused.

Margaret sank on to a plushly upholstered love seat, and thrust her suddenly cold hands under her armpits. Then she took a long, slow breath. 'Perhaps it was thrown out,' she said hopefully.

Mercedes sighed. 'Maybe. More likely it's in one of the attics back at the Manor. I'll call Oriana and ask her to have a rummage, if I can't find it here or at Lowell's.'

'You do that,' Margaret heard herself say faintly, then rung off. She'd have to stop Mercedes getting her hands on that diary, of course. In fact, Mercedes was getting too damn nosy altogether. For a long while she sat on the love seat, her eyes narrowing in temper before violently throwing the mobile at the wall, where it broke and shattered into tiny pieces on the Aubusson rug.

* * *

Oriana could have kissed the grey-muzzled, panting black Labrador.

Connor's friend had arrived only a few minutes ago, and Connor had explained rapidly, but without going into detail, what he wanted Pete to do — namely, get Garbo to go over the house, searching for drugs.

Garbo had willingly obliged, for to him it was a familiar and delightful game. And his nose didn't let him down. He found it within moments, a small white package, hidden in a box of washing powder.

'Better go over the rest of the house, Pete,' Connor said, taking the package from him with obvious distaste. Pete, who'd turned out to be a middle-aged but fit-looking man with salt-and-pepper hair and tired blue eyes, glanced at Oriana curiously, but quickly set the dog off on his search.

The rest of the kitchen proved bare of any more drugs, and when he went out into the hall and through into the living room, Oriana stared at the packet in Connor's big hand. It looked tiny. Insignificant. But she knew its power. In prison, many of her fellow inmates were hooked on stuff just like that, and were willing to trade everything they had in order to be supplied with it.

'Get rid of it,' she said harshly, her disgust obvious.

Connor nodded, went outside, and was gone for about ten minutes. During that time, Oriana heard Pete and the dog go upstairs. And began slowly to relax. For the first time, she felt safe again. Then she heard it. The sound of a car. No sirens, but then a police car on a quiet country lane wouldn't need a siren. Of course, the car could belong to any villager.

Or guest at the hotel. They had to pass by the Manor House all the time. But Oriana *knew* it was a police car.

She was just opening the back door when Connor came through it. He took one look at her and asked harshly, 'What?'

Oriana swallowed hard. 'I think they're here,' she said hoarsely.

Connor didn't need to ask who she meant. He swore and dashed into the hall, looking into the living room. Oriana, following him, said quickly, 'They're upstairs.'

Outside, a car pulled onto the gravel drive. Connor raced to the foot of the stairs, but instead of shouting, gave a long, low whistle. Within moments, man and dog appeared on the landing. 'Scarper,' Connor hissed. 'Out the back.'

With a nod, man and dog raced downstairs and disappeared. As they did so, the front doorbell pealed. Long and hard.

Oriana flinched.

Connor grinned. 'Well, go on, girl. Let 'em in.'

The sight of his grinning face and the cockiness of his voice gave her instant backbone, and she almost smiled too. Then she went to open the door. She was calm but well aware of the ordeal which lay ahead. But she could cope with it. She felt as if she could cope with anything now.

They had a warrant, of course. They went straight to the kitchen. Naturally.

Connor offered to make them tea. There were two of them, both young, both in uniform. They both said no to the tea. One of them glanced at the rather messy kitchen, for Oriana and Connor hadn't put everything back in its place after the search they'd conducted while waiting for Pete. The officer shot them suspicious looks, but Oriana merely gazed back, limpid-eyed and calm.

Connor asked if they might like something stronger.

Twenty minutes and some hard, ugly questions later they finally left. Empty-handed.

With the sound of the retreating police car echoing in their ears, Connor looked at Oriana thoughtfully. He was glad to see that she seemed to have got over her paralysing fear. She looked grim but calm. And he had confidence that she'd stay that way.

'So, I take it things are moving at last?' he said softly.

Oriana nodded. 'Seems like it.' He waited, but she said nothing more and Connor sighed. He understood, to some extent, why she was loath to take him fully into her confidence, and he understood only too well how it was sometimes imperative to play a lone hand. And so far she'd obviously been doing well. They had several leads to go on, including the money trail leading from Frances Greer, which Oriana's private eye was still following up. But he thought the time had come for her to put her cards on the table. He didn't like working in the dark when the fireworks started flying.

'You've upset someone,' he probed gently. Oriana nodded. 'You know who?'

Her eyes glinted. 'Oh yes. I know who.'

'We're on the final home stretch?'

Oriana frowned. Were they? What *would* Margaret do next? Now that her drugs scheme had failed, surely she'd cool it for a while? At least until she had another scheme planned. And in the meantime . . .

She sighed. 'I know you want me to come clean, Connor, but I can't. Not quite yet.' Not whilst Lowell was still mixed up with Margaret. Not while she still had no positive proof. 'But now we know the danger's close, we can take measures, right?' she added nervously.

Connor nodded grimly. 'Too damned right,' he affirmed. 'From now on, I'm going to be watching you like a hawk.'

ELEVEN

When Lowell left Oriana, he walked down the lane slowly, feeling curiously disassociated. In a laurel bush, a blackbird sang beautifully, but he seemed to hear it as if from a distance. The glorious weather was continuing, but the strength of the sun's warmth didn't quite seem to touch him. All he could think of was Oriana, and their love-making. And how it had changed everything; *literally* everything.

He would have to call Margaret and tell her it was over between them. In truth, he didn't think she'd much like it. Although there had certainly been no love between them, Lowell was well aware of Margaret's nature, and he didn't expect the spoilt only daughter of a very rich man to take rejection well. Added to the fact that she was older than him, although still precociously beautiful, and he knew he'd have to be very tactful indeed about what he said. He certainly didn't want to hurt her. For all the woman-of-the-world image she projected, he thought, on more than one occasion, that he'd detected a streak of weakness, a sense of inferiority which ran through her character, making her wildly unpredictable.

Also, Lowell was no fool, and knew exactly why Margaret had been so dead set on him just over four years ago, after her last divorce. She'd needed a young lover to boost her confidence. So when she'd set out to get him, he hadn't put up much of a struggle. Why should he? She wasn't the kind of woman who would be hurt because he couldn't love her. In fact, he'd thought in the early days that she'd have been embarrassed if he *had* fallen for her. She was nothing like Oriana, so there could be no question of her becoming a substitute. And he was a man. He had needs. All in all, it had seemed like an ideal arrangement for both of them. She had her handsome young stud to squire her around, he had a no-strings girlfriend.

But just recently, he knew that it had all begun to change. She'd started to hint about what a good match they'd make. With her money he could buy back the Manor. Oh, she hadn't come out with such an old-fashioned word as 'dowry', but she'd hinted. Even before Oriana had come back, he'd realized that he was going to have to extricate himself from Margaret. Now, after what had just happened, it had become more urgent, that was all.

He was passing Honeysuckle Cottage now, and he paused, looking at it thoughtfully. He needed to talk to Mercedes, about Connor, and the way things were.

Until now, he'd assumed the big blond giant and Oriana had been lovers. Now he knew that wasn't the case. Oriana's virginity had been beyond question. Even now, his body pleasantly aching with remembered passion, he could recall the exact moment when he'd realized that she had saved herself for him.

He supposed he shouldn't have been so surprised. After all, she'd been so young when she was first imprisoned, and had never been the promiscuous sort. And what opportunity to meet men did she have in a women's prison? But when she'd turned up at the Manor with Connor in tow, naturally he'd assumed the worst. As must have Mercedes. Not that it had stopped her falling for him, evidently.

Lowell pushed open the gate and walked up the path, again the loveliness of the cottage garden, the bright scarlet of poppies, the white simplicity of moon daisies, the scattered sky blue of forget-me-nots, all one pace removed from him.

He could still smell Oriana's skin, however. Still feel the soft teasing brush of her breasts against him. The sound of her voice, the rake of her nails. He wondered, vaguely, if he was ever going to come down from cloud nine, and doubted it.

Oriana was back. She was innocent. She was his. For the first time in his life, everything was as it should be. After all the years of pain and denial, it was going to take some getting used to!

He knocked on the door, but there was no answer, although he thought he could hear the shower running upstairs. With a shrug, he turned and went back to the hotel. There was always work to be done there, but for once, he felt too restless to settle down.

Oriana.

He couldn't take his mind off her.

She was innocent. She was. She had to be. He couldn't now bear to contemplate any other possibility. Besides, she had some valid points. How *had* Frances Greer been able to afford to retire to Brighton? And without her evidence, everything else which had convicted Oriana had been purely circumstantial. And Rollo *had* been very up and excited that last summer, as if he had some mischief on his mind. Whatever it was, it could have got him killed. And who had given Oriana enough money to buy the Manor? And why?

He had no answers yet, but he was determined to get them – no matter how close-lipped Oriana wanted to remain. Now that she was back, he was going to make sure she stayed back. Just let anyone, or *anything*, try to come between them. Including Oriana herself!

He thrust aside the folder he was compiling on the possibilities of holding themed weekends at the hotel during the winter, and rang Margaret's number, bracing for an unpleasant time ahead. He'd ask to meet and break it off face to face, of course — but her number was engaged. Thwarted, he paced restlessly to his office window and thought he saw the fair golden head of Oriana in his sister's garden. Yes – it was her. Leaving. With Connor.

Lowell watched them go, his eyes thoughtful, his chin clenched determinedly. He'd have to have a word with Connor, and find out just what was going on there.

For the next ten minutes he tried again to get some work done, but eventually gave up.

He made his way to Honeysuckle Cottage, and as he tapped on the door and walked in he saw Mercedes hang up the phone. She moved to dish up the boxers' afternoon feed, and looked across at him, her eyes wary.

'Hello. What's up?' she said. Then her eyes narrowed. 'You look . . . different,' she added softly.

Lowell smiled slowly. 'Yes,' he agreed. 'I dare say I do. Was that Connor I saw leave a while ago?' he said, changing the subject firmly.

Mercedes nodded and smiled uncertainly as Lowell held up a hand in an appeasing gesture. 'Relax, I haven't come to play the disapproving brother. In fact, rather the opposite.'

'Oh?' Mercedes asked cautiously, putting the dishes to one side and walking to the table. Nevertheless, a warm glow started to ignite in the pit of her stomach. Lowell was all the family she had left now, and she hadn't liked it that he disapproved of Connor. Though she could understand it. But Lowell was looking, well, alive, somehow. And with a start, Mercedes realized that the tense lines which usually marred her brother's handsome face were gone.

'Lowell, what is it?' she breathed, holding out her hand, glad when he took it and sank on to the seat next to her.

'As a matter of fact, I've come to tell you that I think you're right about Connor. About him and Oriana, I mean. That there's something odd about them.'

Mercedes tensed. 'What do you mean?' Did he know that Connor had just left with the snap of Oriana's fingers? Did he know why? What was—?

'Yes. For a start, they're not lovers,' he said firmly. 'You can take it from me. In fact, I think it's about time we sat down, all four of us, and thrashed this thing out once and for all,' Lowell said firmly. And his grey eyes gleamed like polished steel.

Mercedes grinned. When he got that look on his face, she knew nothing would move him. And she would be only too pleased to get things out in the open too. But first things first. With her heart bursting, she clasped his hand strongly. 'What do you mean, they're not lovers? How can you be so sure?'

Lowell gazed back at her calmly. 'Never mind. Just take it from me. They're not sleeping together. So you and Connor shouldn't have any problems.'

Mercedes nodded, but some of her delight faded slowly away. Connor might not be in love with Oriana, but something certainly bound him to her. And whilst it did, she didn't think her future with Connor was going to be as problem-free as her brother seemed to think. Mercedes stiffened her shoulders. Still, she was a big girl now. She would cope. She would fight for Connor, tooth and nail, if need be.

She put the kettle on, finished feeding the dogs, chatted to her brother about her birthday party, which was only two days away now, and was to be held at the hotel, and went through some final arrangements for it. So it was nearly half an hour later before Lowell left, and as he did so, he glanced down the lane towards the Manor, and saw the police cars leaving.

* * *

Oriana looked up as she heard the front door open. Connor had just gone out the back door, to make sure Pete and Garbo had got away clean, and she felt herself tensing up. Had the police come back? But a moment later, she saw Lowell's dark head appear, and all her previous angst fled. Her face softened. She smiled. 'Hello,' she said softly.

Lowell smiled back. He hadn't expected to return so soon. He'd thought he'd have more time to sort things out in his own mind before seeing her again. Now, all he wanted to do was take her in his arms and hold her, although at the same time, he felt an instinctive need to keep his distance. He still felt distinctly destabilized by the events of the last few weeks. And of the last few hours in particular.

'I thought I saw the police leave,' he said, keeping his tone of voice to one of mild curiosity.

Oriana's face tightened. Damn! She instantly considered lying to him, but she was so sick of lies. It felt as if she'd played nothing but a lying game ever since she was sixteen. 'Yes. They came because they'd got a tip-off that I was some sort of local drug pusher,' she said flatly, then could have cried with relief and love when she saw the shock and anger flood his face.

'What a load of bullshit,' Lowell said hoarsely. 'You? Never in a million years.'

His whole-hearted defence of her made her want to sing, and she laughed. 'Well, once you give a dog a bad name,' she said, shrugging lightly. 'Needless to say, they came, they searched, and they went away again with nothing more incriminating than a packet of baking powder to analyse.'

Lowell laughed. He couldn't help it. He didn't know anyone quite like Oriana.

She laughed too. Her eyes became sapphires, hard with desire, on fire with longing. The look she gave him spoke volumes, and Lowell felt his body harden and leap in response.

'Oriana, I—'

'It's all right, they're gone.' Connor's cheerful voice made both of them jump and look to the corridor, and when Oriana looked back at Lowell, she could see, with a pang, that he was already withdrawing from her.

What had he been about to say?

Lowell, who'd been going to blurt out — just like the famous song promised — something stupid like 'I love you', turned and watched instead, closed-faced but no longer hostile, as Connor walked in.

The big man took one look at Oriana, stiffened and spun around. For a moment, Lowell sensed something in his movement, like a cat poised ready to spring, but the next second, Connor recognized him and was nodding cordially.

'Good afternoon, Mr Seton,' Connor said blandly.

'Call me Lowell. If you're going to court my sister, I think first names are called for, don't you?'

Connor grinned. It was a friendly grin, and held not a little relief at the relationship being out in the open, and Lowell knew, in that instant, that he had found a friend. Perhaps a very good friend. It was odd how he could loathe the man one moment yet feel so mellow towards him the next. But he knew why, of course. He was after Mercedes, his sister, not Oriana, the woman he loved.

That tended to make a difference!

Lowell nodded, glanced at Oriana, made a vague 'about to leave' gesture, and she stirred unhappily. Why had Connor come back just then? He'd been about to say something to her – something important. She was sure of it.

'I'll see you on Saturday, if not before then,' he said, and Oriana frowned vaguely. 'Mercedes' birthday party?' he prompted.

Oriana clapped a hand to her mouth. She'd forgotten all about it! She'd have to go into Oxford and get a new outfit. 'Oh yes, of course.'

'Do you want me to pick you up?' he asked softly.

Oriana paused, hesitant. Did this mean he'd already broken it off with Margaret? Or that he at least intended to before then? Her heart leapt at the thought, but she knew she had to be careful. She glanced uncertainly at Connor. She knew he'd want to be seen as Mercedes' date. And heaven knew, Oriana wanted all the world to know that she and Lowell were together. But . . .

'It's all right,' she said reluctantly. 'Connor and I can walk up together.'

Lowell nodded stiffly. 'Right.'

Oriana watched him go, stubbornly holding on to her previous sense of happiness, but it wasn't easy.

* * *

The Dower House Hotel ballroom looked beautiful. Flowers, both from the local florist and from Mercedes' own garden, had been arranged in huge vases. Candles, flickering in jewel-coloured glass sconces of ruby red, emerald green, blue, gold and deep amethyst, added to the discreet lighting of the electric chandeliers. In one corner, a small band played middle-of-the-road classics, some popular jazz, a few sixties pop favourites and assorted dance numbers.

A bar, overflowing with everything from expensive champagne and intricate cocktails to the locally brewed Hook Norton ale made sure the guests were kept happy.

In the foyer, Mercedes, a vision in gold and white, greeted the guests. It was nearly nine, and already the hotel was full. Her friends from the dog show circuit, villagers, family and other more casual acquaintances had piled presents for her on the table behind her, and now milled around inside, buffet tables, groaning with delicacies, tempting them away from the official greeting line. Mercedes, who was looking out for only one special guest, encouraged them to eat, drink and be merry.

Lowell was inside, looking absolutely stunning in a black tuxedo. Mercedes had noticed that Margaret was clinging to him like a limpet, and was sure she'd felt a tension between them when they'd arrived. Obviously something was wrong.

But then she saw Connor, and all thoughts about her brother's complicated love life fled. The fact that Oriana walked in with him, looking absolutely breathtaking in a layered ballgown of ice blue, fading to pale lilac and silver, meant nothing to her.

She had eyes only for him.

He looked wonderful in a white dinner jacket, hunter-green bow tie, impeccably creased trousers and black shoes. He'd even had his untidy hair trimmed, though it was still too long for fashion's comfort, and remained untamed around his leonine head. His eyes met hers the moment he walked into the foyer.

With a discreet murmur, Oriana took herself off. At the entrance to the crowded room, she hesitated and took a deep breath. She'd always known this was going to be hard. It was one thing for the village, the villagers, and society at large to know that she was back; it was another thing altogether to flaunt the knowledge in their faces.

As she stood in the doorway, looking around, there was no embarrassing lull in the conversation. The band played on, people continued dancing, chatting or drinking. The vast majority of people, in fact — especially the hotel guests who'd wandered in, and the younger element, who would have been too young to know or care about the trial — had no idea who she was.

But Oriana knew some were watching her. Some of the talk had veered to her. Some were wondering . . .

Then Lowell was there. The midnight blackness of the tuxedo echoed the raven of his hair. His grey eyes, as soft as molten pewter, ran over her lovingly.

The dress, which left her shoulders and arms bare, hugged her breasts and waist, before falling to her feet in a bell shape. With her curly fair hair caught up in intricate whorls, laced through with live forget-me-nots and flowers of purple honesty, she looked as beautiful as summer itself.

'Want to dance?' he asked softly.

Oriana nodded. She didn't look around to see if Margaret Wright was there. She didn't want to know. She didn't want to hear the whispers or gasps of surprise, either, as Lowell Seton took the supposed murderess of his brother into his arms and led her onto the dance floor. She didn't want anything to mar this moment. This wonderful, perfect moment.

The band began to play the theme from the film *Love Story*. She flowed into his arms, resting her cheek against his shoulder and let him lead her where he would. Let them all stare.

* * *

Outside, in the now near-deserted foyer, oblivious to the scandal Lowell and Oriana were creating within, Mercedes continued to gaze at Connor.

'What, have you never seen a dog's dinner all dressed up before?' he asked teasingly, stepping back and indicating his suit. 'And here I was, thinking I scrubbed up rather well. Certainly good enough not to embarrass the birthday girl.'

Mercedes let him ramble on, an indulgent look on her face. 'You know damned well you're the best-looking man in the place,' she scoffed.

'You're the most beautiful woman here,' he said seriously.

Mercedes laughed. 'Now that the mutual admiration society has convened, perhaps we can cut out the preliminaries.'

'Too right,' he said. 'Let's cut straight to the important things. First, the present.'

So saying, he whipped out a small gold foil-wrapped parcel, which had been concealed in his hip pocket. Mercedes swallowed hard, unwrapped the small box and opened it. Inside was a silver-and-onyx pendant of an intricate, ancient-looking Celtic design. She knew at once the silver would look spectacular with her colouring, and the gold-and-white dress she was wearing.

She removed the gold choker which was already round her neck, laughingly dropped it into an urn housing a thriving goosefoot plant, then turned her back to him, holding up her wavy black tresses. 'Put it on, please,' she said softly, holding her breath as she felt his fingers brush against the back of her neck.

He fastened the tiny clasp quickly, and with none of the fumbling she might have expected from a man with such big fingers. When she turned around, the pendant nestled in the hollow at her throat, just above the V-shaped bodice of her dress.

Connor slowly relaxed. 'When I saw it, I thought it would look good on you. Pagan, and full of contradiction. Black and silver. Night and light.'

'Are you calling me a witch?' she asked, intrigued.

'Oh, in the old days, there'd be no doubt about it,' he said softly. 'Someone as beautiful as you, with all this mass of midnight-coloured hair. You'd soon have been burned at the stake.' He lifted a long tress of her hair, raised it to his lips, and kissed it.

Their eyes met. 'About the other day,' he said softly. 'There was an emergency. I *had* to leave with Oriana, but it meant nothing more than that. I hated to leave you. You know that, don't you?' Mercedes nodded. 'You forgive me?' he pressed.

'Yes,' she murmured. Gone was the feeling of resentment. Gone were all the remaining doubts.

'Good,' Connor said, 'because I think we're going somewhere, you and I. Don't you?'

Mercedes looked up at him and smiled, tears of happiness brightening her eyes. This was, without doubt, her best birthday. Ever.

Those already shocked by the togetherness of Lowell and Oriana were further shocked by the togetherness of Oriana's live-in lover and Mercedes Seton as they entered the room. Obviously there was something massive in the air tonight, and an infectious excitement seemed to catch hold of the room; people danced more closely, drank more deeply, laughed and felt more alive.

Of those watching the two couples, Margaret Wright was the only one who felt no sense of surprise, no sense of intrigue. Only rage.

Lowell had called for her an hour ago, and had broken things off between them. Even though she'd been expecting it, and knew she merely had to ride it out until she could think of another way of getting rid of Oriana, it had still taken her unawares.

Still, she had played the scene well. The right amount of regret, mixed with rueful promises that she had always known the day would come. A laughing avowal that she was perfectly all right with carrying on and attending the party. When had Lowell ever known her to miss a good party? Besides, she was all dressed up. The latest design from Paris, a mini-cocktail dress in peacock blue, simply deserved an airing.

She'd caught the flash of surprise in his eyes that she was taking it so well, coupled with a wariness which made her want to laugh out loud. Oh yes. He would do well to be careful. She would make him pay, all right. In her own way. But she could wait.

She still had no idea what had gone wrong with her drugs plan. By rights, Oriana Foster should now be back behind bars, not dancing in the arms of someone else's property. But that, too, would have to wait. Right now, she had another fish to fry.

Mercedes, when she'd arrived, had told her she'd been unable to find Rollo's diary in either the Dower House or her own cottage, and would ask Oriana later to look in the attics of the Manor. And Margaret simply couldn't allow *that* to happen.

Mercedes, as the hostess, had, perforce, to circulate. It was difficult to be constantly polite, even in the best of circumstances, but when all she wanted to do was go back to Connor, to be held in those strong arms again, enclosed in his massive embrace, and dance the night away, it was almost impossible.

When she felt a piece of paper being slipped into her hand, she jumped and looked around, but it was impossible to see, in the crush, who'd passed it on.

Lowell was by the French windows, talking to Oriana; Margaret was nearby, but at the bar. And she couldn't see Connor.

Curious, she walked over to one of the flickering candles and read the little note.

Meet me in the pool room. Now!

It wasn't signed, but she smiled and bit her lower lip. Who else but Connor could have written it? She crumpled up the note, let it fall into a waste-paper bin and looked around, a shade guiltily, a shade defiantly, at her guests.

Connor was still nowhere to be seen. Obviously not. He had to be waiting for her in the pool room.

She moved slowly to the far side of the room, slipping out and taking off her gold heels as she walked down the narrow back corridor which twisted and turned and led to the rear of the house.

Here, Lowell had cunningly turned the old orangery into an indoor pool area, keeping some of the orange blossom plants and all the old white-painted wrought-iron garden furniture to create a gothic-style indoor pool-cum-conservatory.

The pool had been closed for the night, of course, as it was now approaching midnight and, as she peered inside, all seemed dark. A moon, shining through the glass walls, illuminated the pool, turning it into an onyx and silver rectangle. It reminded her of Connor's gift, and she fingered her pendant lovingly as she walked inside.

She could see no one and nothing. 'Connor,' she half-whispered, half-hissed. 'Where are you?' She let the door close behind her, blocking out the sound of the party.

'Hey, I'm over here!' she whispered. Where was the big romantic fool?

She walked closer, skirting the edge of the pool, peering into the flowering greenery.

'Connor,' she called again. Then yelped as something tripped her. She wasn't sure what it was – a low piece of furniture which she hadn't seen in the darkness, perhaps. Something fairly solid, anyway, catching the back of her legs and pitching her forward.

It all happened in less than a second, and then she was in the water. It closed over her like a smothering blanket, avid and eager, almost playful. As if inviting her to join in the joke. But it wasn't funny. Mercedes couldn't swim.

TWELVE

She managed to grab a lungful of air just before she went under. It was an instinctive gasp, taken as the coolness of the water hit her, but shock made her expel at least half of it as she submerged. Panic swept over her as the sensations of water, its buoyancy and clogging, heavy presence, engulfed her.

Like most people who loved the land, dogs and all things earthy, she'd never much taken to the water. Whereas Lowell could swim like a fish, she had never bothered to learn.

The chlorine in the water stung her eyes, but she forced herself to keep them open. Up. She had to get up, somehow. She moved her arms, but they felt sluggish. She wanted desperately to breathe, but knew that she couldn't. Somehow, she broke the surface and took a deep gulp, her arms flailing in her panic. Now that she was on the surface again, she was determined not to sink once more. But she was already doing so. Her chin and then her mouth were under. Frantically she tried to thrust her head above the water, but that only seemed to make her sink faster. She thrashed, knowing that she was probably doing everything wrong, but for the moment she couldn't think.

She only knew she was under water again. Sound felt clogged, as if her ears were packed with cotton wool, and the only thing she could hear was the fast, panicky beat of her heart. Her life, unlike popular belief, didn't flash in front of her eyes. Instead she felt pain, mostly in her ribs, as she struggled to hold her breath.

She couldn't do this. She couldn't die like this, at her own birthday party. Not now that she'd found Connor!

She hit the surface again, but barely, and wondered in despair what it was that had made her come to the top. If only she could figure it out, she could keep on doing it. She looked to the side of the pool, which seemed ridiculously close. All she had to do was move a few feet and she would be clinging safely to the side. But how?

She recalled watching Lowell swimming in the Cherwell as a boy, using overarm strokes. They'd seemed to propel him easily through the water, but when she finally got up the nerve to thrust her arm firmly into the air, she only began to sink again. She managed a scream this time, but it was more a sound of hopeless despair and growing rage than a serious call for help. She didn't think anyone at the party would be able to hear her, and no one was going to chance by the pool room.

But where was Connor?

As she went under yet again, Mercedes vaguely realized that there was something else that was wrong. Something to do with Connor, the note, her fall. But then the hateful water was dragging her under again, and her thoughts concentrated, shriekingly, on her lack of air once more.

Connor wondered where Mercedes had gone. He'd just stepped into the hall to retrieve her gold choker, the security man in him loath to leave something so valuable in such an impromptu hiding place, and when he'd come back he'd thought he'd seen her on the far side of the room, heading for one of the side doors.

Now she was gone.

Curious, he followed her route to the door, found it open and walked outside. He was in a narrow corridor, obviously once used by servants to carry food from the kitchens. But there was no sign of Mercedes. Intrigued, he followed the passage down, and thought he heard a faint cry. He stopped, listening hard. But with the sound of the music and party behind him, he wasn't sure. Instinct made him carry on, however, walking faster now, until he abruptly came upon the huge kitchens. One quick look showed caterers and hotel staff busy at work, but still no sign of Mercedes. Over the clattering of pots and pans, he listened again, but could hear nothing. Shrugging, he let the door shut behind him and looked around.

At the end of the dog-leg corridor he could see a glass door, but beyond it was nothing but darkness. He was about to turn and go back to the party, when something, some movement out of the corner of his eye, made him turn quickly to the glass door again. Some slim flash of paleness in the dark. Probably moonlight and shadows playing tricks. Still, he had nothing better to do.

He walked down, pushed open the unlocked door and found himself in a pool house. And a hot house. The scent of orange blossom and chlorinated water fought pleasantly with each other.

Connor looked up first, noting the play of moonlight through the glass dome on the profusion of plants, then down into the water itself. And yelled.

'*Mercedes!*'

He dived into the pool fully clothed and still wearing his shoes, ignoring all the rules and protocols which he would normally have followed during a rescue attempt of a drowning person. But now, all he was thinking of was getting her out of there. For he had no doubt at all that the mass of dark hair, floating like raven river weed just below the water's surface, belonged to Mercedes. His huge, powerful body plummeted downward, rock-solid arm muscles propelling him to her in just two strokes.

Mercedes felt something warm and strong wrap around her waist, and for a second instinctively panicked, kicking out. Then she felt herself moving upwards, and a moment later, she was breathing blissful air again.

Mercedes gasped and began to cry. She furiously told herself to stop it, but she couldn't.

Connor, one hand firmly under her chin, towed them to the side, then, with one push of his spread hand under her bottom, rocketed her out and onto the side of the pool. Mercedes slumped along the mosaic tiles and gasped, shivering with reaction. In a second, he'd hauled himself out beside her, and was kneeling over her. He carefully turned her over.

'Did you swallow any water?' he asked, all too aware of the problems caused by secondary drowning.

Mercedes shook her head. 'No. Not m-much,' she managed to choke out, around her sobs.

'Are you sure?' he asked urgently. Sometimes, victims could be saved from drowning, but they might already have inhaled water into their lungs, which then couldn't function properly. It was not unknown for someone, in such a state, to literally drown while sitting on a sofa in front of a TV.

'I'm calling a doctor,' he said, but Mercedes reached up and grabbed him. Her hands, clutching the material of his trousers, were like a vice. 'Wait. Just hold me a minute, will you?'

Connor pulled her to him and held her tight, but not too tight, rocking her back and forth and letting her cry out her shock, mumbling over and over that he loved her, that he was never letting her go. He wasn't sure that she heard.

Later, after she was feeling calmer, she rubbed a hand shakily across her face, 'I must look a mess,' she hiccoughed.

'You look gorgeous,' he told her, somewhat less than honestly. Her mascara had run, and her lovely gown clung to her like a wilted buttercup. His necklace still hung around her neck however, and he felt his heart shudder at how close he had come to actually losing her.

What was she doing in the pool house? he wanted to demand, shaking her, and telling her off for scaring him so thoroughly. But now was not the time. She looked all done in. 'Come on, let's get you upstairs and call out a doctor. I'll get Lowell – he must have a free bedroom available.'

Mercedes nodded, and felt utterly bereft for the scant minute he was gone. When he came back, with her white-faced brother and an equally worried-looking Oriana in tow, she immediately held her hands out to him. She didn't care if it was pathetic. She wanted him to hold her again.

Wordlessly he picked her up, then glanced at Lowell, who nodded. 'I'll call our GP,' he said. 'She can have my room tonight – top floor, turn left at the stairs. It's the only door marked "Private". I'll be up in a minute.' Connor nodded, and Lowell watched them go. In that instant, he couldn't think of any other man he would trust with his sister's safety and care more than Connor.

Oriana also watched them go, then glanced into the pool. She looked puzzled. As Mercedes' oldest friend, she knew of her friend's aversion to the water.

Just what had she been doing in here?

The guests weren't told of Mercedes' mishaps and it was gone two before the last of them began to leave: villagers to go home and gossip about Oriana and Lowell; hotel guests to the comfort and luxury of their rooms; Margaret Wright to return home, once again thwarted. And now, badly scared.

They were all in Lowell's room, a bedside lamp turned on to give a pearly light. The doctor had been and gone and, after listening to her lungs, pronounced her safe from harm. She had refused the sedative he'd prescribed, however, and she and Connor were now amiably bickering about it, as Lowell and Oriana looked on indulgently.

'I'll have no trouble sleeping, believe me,' Mercedes was grumbling. Then she shot Connor a wicked look. 'Especially if you sleep next to me.'

Connor pulled a comically shocked look. 'I will not,' he said, raising his voice to a shocked squeak. 'The very idea. Hussy! No, you need to rest. I'll stay just outside, if you like. Or sleep on a chair in here.'

Mercedes pouted. With her hair now dry, her face clean of make-up, and enveloped in a pair of her brother's borrowed pyjamas, she looked like a little girl who'd just been scolded.

'How did you come to fall in the pool anyway?' It was Lowell who finally asked the question, and Mercedes gave him a fond, rueful look.

'Beats me,' she said, trying to remember. The thing was, the events were beginning to seem a little vague, as if they had happened long ago, and far away. 'I remember feeling something hard against my legs, fairly low down. So perhaps I stumbled against one of the deck chairs?'

Oriana frowned, but said nothing.

Lowell shook his head exasperatedly. 'You muffin,' he said tenderly.

Mercedes stuck out her tongue at him.

'What were you doing there in the first place?' Connor chided. 'That's what I want to know.'

'Oh that. I got a note,' Mercedes said, yawning hugely. 'I thought it was from you.'

Connor went very still, then slowly shook his head. He forced himself to smile. 'Nope. Not from me. Tell me, have you got many prospective lovers lurking about in the under-growth that I need to know about?' he teased. But when he glanced over her head, his eyes, when he met Oriana's grim gaze, were as hard as flint. A knowing look passed between them.

'Maybe,' Mercedes said teasingly, then yawned again. 'Maybe I have a whole football team of them lined up, ready to give you a run for your money.'

Her eyes drooped helplessly.

'It's time we left her to sleep,' Lowell said, in a decisive, big-brother way which not even Connor would have argued with. He nodded, kissed Mercedes' forehead – much to her disgust – and together all three of them left the room.

Oriana moved away tactfully, leaving the two men to talk. Obviously it was decided that Connor would leave and Lowell would spend the night in the chair for, a moment or two later, he joined her at the head of the stairs.

Oriana looked back, waved a little forlornly at Lowell, who watched her with enigmatic grey eyes, then turned and followed Connor out into the early hours of the morning. He waited until they were in the lane before speaking.

'You know someone tried to kill her, don't you?' he said flatly. He turned to look at her and thought that if she tried to stall him again, it was all over between them. He'd resign, and to hell with professional ethics.

But she nodded. 'Yes. I think so, too,' she agreed simply.

'And you know who. And this time you're going to tell me,' he said grimly.

Oriana nodded. And told him.

* * *

It had only just gone nine o'clock the next morning when Connor and Oriana pulled up to the impressive double-gated entrance to Penny Farthing, the impressive mock-Tudor mansion where the Wrights had lived for the past decade. Connor got out and pushed the button below the electronic gate box. In the car, Oriana heard a muted voice answer, and heard Connor reply.

'Miss Oriana Foster and a Mr Connor O'Dell to see Sir Frederick Wright, please.'

There was another mumble from the box.

'No, we don't have an appointment.'

Oriana waited and a few moments later there was a small click and a whirr, and the gates began to open. Connor moved back quickly behind the wheel, and then they were off. They parked outside the big oak doors, and Oriana glanced over at him.

'You all right?'

Connor looked at her grimly, but understood her. He took a deep breath and nodded. 'I've got everything under control, yes.'

Oriana was relieved. She didn't think she'd ever want to see Connor when he was angry and out of control.

They went to the door, which was opened before they could reach it by a butler. Middle-aged, blank-eyed, faultlessly polite, he led them through into the study. There, an old man was already rising to his feet to greet them. With a shock of white hair, his back becoming stooped with age, he still held a remnant of his former glory. But his hands shook a little as he put down his paper, and in his eyes was a defeat which was impossible to disguise.

Oriana knew at once that he'd been expecting them. Oh, not today, perhaps, but sometime.

'Please, won't you sit down. Tea? Coffee?' he asked, his voice wavering with an old man's tremor.

'Not for me, thank you,' Oriana said. Connor likewise shook his head. The butler, without asking, withdrew.

'Please, sit down, Sir Frederick,' Oriana said, wondering why her voice came out sounding so soft and concerned.

She'd imagined this meeting, of course, many times, in her head. During her long sleepless nights in the cells, which she'd sometimes had to share with three other girls, she'd considered this moment. And always, in her imaginings, she'd been dominant, scornful, full of righteous wrath and anger. But now, in reality, looking at the old man who was the cause of all her troubles, she was almost shocked to find herself feeling sorry for him. It puzzled her, and made her unsure. Not that it showed in her unwavering blue gaze.

Fred looked at her, a little surprised to find her still so beautiful. Still so young. But of course, she had been little more than a child when she'd been convicted. He sighed heavily and sank thankfully onto the chair, more falling into it than lowering himself down.

Oriana took the armchair opposite him and Connor, after a moment's hesitation, moved to the sofa, just a little to the right. It gave both of them an uninterrupted view of the old man. Like Oriana, Connor was feeling some of his antipathy leaching away. The enemy was old and exhausted after all. It was hard to summon up an enthusiasm for what was to come, even though both he and Oriana knew it had to be done.

'You don't look surprised to see me, Sir Frederick,' Oriana said, and the old man waved a hand, almost angrily.

'Please, don't call me "Sir",' he stunned her by saying. 'It's a title they gave me years ago, before I realized how little I deserved it. Just call me . . .' And there he had to stop. Stumped. For they wouldn't want to call him by his first name – they were hardly friends. And 'Mr Wright' sounded, somehow, absurd.

He sighed and shook his head.

'Why did you give me the two million pounds?' Oriana said, the fantastic words, in that genteel, book-lined room, sounding exotic and bizarre.

But Fred only smiled, making no attempt to demur. 'What else could I do?' he said simply.

'You could have stood up for me at the trial,' Oriana said harshly, but when he looked at her, surprise for the first time showing in his face, she felt her first frisson of unease. Had she got it all wrong?

'I didn't know, at the time of your trial, that you needed standing up for,' Fred said. 'If I had . . .' and then his voice tailed away as he forced himself to take a good hard look at himself. Yes. If he *had* known at the time, just what *would* he have done? He'd like to think that he would have done the decent thing, but now he was not so sure.

'You didn't know?' Oriana said softly, shaking her head. 'All this time I thought it must have been you. *You* who killed Rollo, until I realized that Margaret was in on it too. But that wasn't how it was, was it?' she breathed.

And Fred shook his head. 'No. I had nothing to do with young Rollo's death,' he said sadly.

'His murder, you mean.' Connor spoke for the first time, and the old man flinched. Connor forced himself not to feel guilty, and Fred looked at him, making a visible effort to brace himself. To show some of his former spunk. Eventually, he nodded.

'You're quite right, of course,' he said at last. 'Let's call a spade a spade. I had nothing to do with Rollo's murder.'

'But you found out who did, didn't you?' Oriana pressed. 'When was it? When you put the money in my name?' It had been some years into her prison sentence when that smuggled letter had told her about her new fortune. 'How did you find out?' she asked flatly. 'How did you discover that your daughter had killed Rollo Seton?' She forced herself to speak it out loud, mindful of Connor's lecture on the hidden microphone which was taped to her shoulder, now recording every word of their conversation.

'It was by accident,' Fred said, his voice a bare mumble, but Connor had assured her that the equipment was the best. It could, as he had so unprepossessingly put it, pick up a fly's cough at a hundred yards.

'We were arguing about . . . something,' he said lamely.

'Money?' Oriana asked.

Fred sighed. 'Yes. Money. With Margaret, it's always money. She'd just got her first – no, second – divorce. Her husband hadn't been as generous as she'd expected, so she asked for a rise in her allowance from me. I was, frankly, worried. It was during her gambling phase, you see. She was losing hundreds of thousands in Monte Carlo and . . . But you don't want to hear this,' he said, shame flooding over him as Oriana's blue eyes flickered.

'Of course she doesn't,' it was Connor who spoke. 'Whilst Margaret was living it up, Oriana was serving time in a women's prison for a crime your daughter had committed.'

Fred flinched, but said nothing in defence, and Oriana shot Connor a warning look.

Connor nodded reluctantly. They'd agreed that she'd do all the running – after all, this was her moment – but thoughts of Mercedes drowning kept making his blood threaten to boil. He curled his hands around the chair's arms, and forced himself to breathe deeply.

'So she wanted more money, and you said no,' Oriana continued calmly. 'Then what?'

'Then she said that I should be more grateful. That it was her money as much as mine. That she'd worked just as hard for it, if not harder. Had got her hands dirty.' Fred paused, and swallowed painfully.

His chest was feeling tight again. A dull pain throbbed there warningly, but he ignored it. 'I asked her just what that was supposed to mean, and then she told me. Just blurted it out. So defiant. By then, of course, she was furious, but when she told me she'd killed Rollo Seton, she looked almost triumphant. Proud of herself. It made me feel sick.'

The old man shook his head. 'I can't say more. I won't.'

Oriana bit her lip. Part of her didn't want to badger him, but she knew she had to.

'So instead of going to the authorities and getting me released from prison, you decided to give me a huge amount of money instead,' she said, doing nothing to hide the disgust in her voice. 'Surely you knew I'd much rather have had my freedom?'

'Of course I knew,' Fred whispered, appalled. He leaned forward and cupped his hands against his face, a broken, tired, ill old man. 'But what could I do?' He slowly lowered his hands and looked at Oriana pitifully. 'She's my only child. I couldn't just . . .' He shook his head. 'I know I can't expect you of all people to understand, but please believe me, I just couldn't betray her. I'm sorry. So sorry. I've tried to make it up to you, and the Setons. I've changed my will — disinheriting Margaret, and leaving the bulk of my estate to be divided between yourself and Mercedes and Lowell Seton. What else can I do?' he appealed.

He was breathing heavily now, and Oriana was becoming alarmed about his colour. She just couldn't go on with it, but Connor, seeing her pity, stepped in. 'You can tell us what it was all about,' he said forcefully. It was the one thing Oriana and he still didn't know. Why? Why had Margaret killed Rollo? How had his death profited the Wrights?

But when Fred looked at him, Connor could tell that he wasn't going to talk. Even before he began shaking his head,

Connor was getting to his feet, a slow, furious burn welling up inside him.

'Do you know what your precious daughter did last night?' he hissed. 'She tried to kill Mercedes. Tell me,' he said, ignoring Fred's sudden cry of disbelief and pain, 'just what has she got against the Seton family?'

Fred Wright leaned back in his chair, shaking his head. Oriana didn't like the way he clutched his hand to his chest. 'Connor,' she said sharply.

He looked at her, his face tight with frustrated fury. She shook her head.

'How can you defend him?' Connor hissed. 'You, who's suffered the most?'

Oriana walked across to him and took one of his tense hands in her own. 'Yes, I suffered,' she said softly. 'And I used to think that nothing could have been worse than what happened to me. But look at him, Connor,' she said softly, and they both glanced back at the old man, sagging in his chair. His face was the colour of suet, his eyes receded deep into their sockets and full of pain. 'Perhaps having a beloved child turn out to be so bad is far worse than any amount of years spent in prison. Besides' – she patted the tiny electronic lump on her shoulder – 'we've got enough. Yes?'

He looked at her long and hard. Then slowly relaxed. 'Yes,' he agreed. Then added under his breath, 'I hope Lowell Seton realizes what a lucky man he is to have someone like you.'

Outside, they climbed back into the car, emotionally exhausted but relieved.

'Well, the end's in sight,' Connor said, as they drove back towards Nether Dene. 'I'll take the recording to a friend of mine at Thames Valley nick if you like. I'll be able to cut through the red tape a bit quicker than you.'

Oriana nodded. 'OK.'

'Unless you want the satisfaction of walking into the police station yourself and letting them have it, right between the eyes.' Oriana laughed but shook her head. In truth, she had nothing against the police. Given the circumstances, and the mountain of testimony which seemed to prove her guilt, she had never blamed the police for her plight.

'No, you can do it,' she said. 'I never want to see a police station again, believe me.'

As they drove down the narrow country lane towards the village, Connor sighed. 'Remember what I told you about the recording? Technically it was illegal, and will be useless in a court of law. So don't expect them to magically arrest Margaret just yet. But it'll be enough to set the ball rolling with the appeal against your conviction, and petition to gain a pardon. And now that they know where to look, they'll find the real proof they need.'

'Your PIs have come through on the money trail, right?'

Oriana grinned. That was true. She'd had a courier-delivered message from them at 7.30 that morning, confirming they could trace Frances Greer's 'inheritance' to one of Margaret Wright's Cayman Island accounts.

As he pulled up outside the Manor, and Oriana climbed out, he leaned across the steering wheel. 'After I've been to Kidlington and seen the cops, I'm going back to Penny Farthing. I want to keep a close eye on our little Miss Wright from now on.'

Oriana laughed. 'Sounds like a good idea to me,' she said feelingly.

But even as she spoke, back at her own home, Margaret Wright was climbing into her car. And in the rear, she had a lethal crossbow and a set of bolts to match.

THIRTEEN

Oriana watched Connor drive away, but felt too restless to go into the empty Manor House and twiddle her thumbs. After her talk with Fred, she sensed things were moving, and needed company. Talk. Distraction. Besides, she wanted to spread the good news. She smiled grimly as she walked down the lane and turned into Mercedes' cottage. Connor had already told her that Mercedes had insisted on going back to her place that morning, assuring him she felt fine; and besides, she'd said, the dogs needed her. And when her old friend answered her knock, Oriana could see that she did indeed look fine.

In fact, she looked radiant.

'Oriana, come in. I was wanting a word with you,' Mercedes said, standing back and ushering her into the kitchen.

Oriana looked at her, a shade warily. 'You seem in a good mood this morning. Considering what happened last night.'

Mercedes waved a hand in the air. 'Oh, who cares about last night,' she said, making Oriana's jaw drop. She'd nearly died, and who *cared*?

'Connor came to the hotel this morning to see how I was. We had a long talk – Lowell, Connor and me. A real heart-to-heart. Didn't he tell you?'

Oriana shook her head. No, he definitely *hadn't* told her. But then, perhaps he thought she didn't need the distraction. Knowing about their upcoming interview with Fred Wright, and its huge importance to them both, he probably thought that she needed to concentrate on the matter in hand. Something she'd hardly have been able to do if she'd been thinking about Lowell.

'Oh,' Mercedes said, a worried frown tugging at her dark brows. 'I thought he'd have told you. I hope I haven't got him in trouble. He told me, you see – about you hiring him as a bodyguard. About there being nothing between you. Ever.'

And Mercedes looked so wonderfully happy that Oriana couldn't help but smile. Who could blame Connor for jumping the gun, and without her permission, when it made her old friend so happy? 'I'm sorry about the misunderstanding,' Oriana said. 'If I'd known you and Connor were going to take one look at each other and fall like the proverbial ton of bricks, I'd have chosen someone else for the job.'

Mercedes grinned. 'Ah, but then we'd never have met.'

'True! So all's well that ends well. That reminds me – I have news.'

And she quickly told her about the interview with Fred that morning. Halfway through it, Mercedes began to turn pale, and slowly sat at the table, her eyes huge. When Oriana had finished, Mercedes shook her head.

'But . . . Sir Freddy? And Margaret. I mean . . . why?'

Oriana shook her head ruefully. 'I don't know why. It's the one thing he wouldn't tell us. Oh, he admitted that he found out it was Margaret who'd really killed Rollo, and that's why he gave me so much money.' And realizing that Lowell hadn't told her about the money, Oriana explained about her mysterious benefactor. 'Although, of course, I thought it must be Fred Wright who'd put the money in my name the moment I got out of prison and learned that it was really true,' Oriana finished.

'But why?' Mercedes asked, puzzled.

Oriana laughed wryly. 'Well, it didn't take Sherlock Holmes to figure it out, did it?' she said. 'Apart from anything else, who do I know with that kind of money? Who lived in the area? Who knew your family, the Setons? Unless I was to believe that some nameless, crazy billionaire had seen my face in the papers, fallen in love from a distance, and decided to lavish a fortune on me, it had to be Frederick Wright.'

Mercedes nodded slowly. 'OK. But why didn't you do something about it the moment you came out?'

Oriana looked at her levelly. 'Like what? Confront him? What if he'd denied it? The solicitor he'd got to act as a go-between would never break his confidence. What then? Go to the press with such a wild tale? Would they believe a convicted murderess? Besides, what sort of crazies might I have attracted if it became known I was wealthy?' Oriana shuddered. 'No thank you. The only thing I could do was to entrench myself at Nether Dene and start trying to find out why Fred Wright wanted Rollo dead. To ask questions and see what crawled out of the woodwork. But I knew that would be dangerous, hence your Connor.'

Mercedes grinned. She liked the sound of that. *Her* Connor.

'OK. So you began to poke around,' Mercedes said. 'Met me and Lowell, and—' She put a sudden, appalled hand to her mouth. 'Margaret and Lowell,' she whispered. 'Oh, Oriana!'

Oriana flinched, but nodded with amazing calm. 'Yes, I hadn't been in the village for more than two minutes before the word reached me. Lowell and Margaret were an item. At first, I couldn't so much as look at Margaret. Not because I suspected her — I wasn't sure of her involvement then — but just because I couldn't bear to look at the woman who had Lowell when . . .' She trailed off helplessly.

'It should have been you,' Mercedes finished for her. And reached out to take her hand, for a moment, in mute sympathy. Then her face tightened.

'We have to tell Lowell. When he finds out it was Margaret who killed Rollo . . .' Mercedes looked, aghast, at Oriana, who was grim-faced. Her jaw jutted out at a pugnacious angle. Her eyes glinted, as if made of diamond chips.

'I know,' Oriana said, her voice like lead. 'It'll make him sick to his stomach. But I won't let him brood on it; I won't let it destroy him, Mercy. I won't.'

Looking into her friend's blazing blue eyes, Mercedes knew that she wouldn't. At last, Lowell had someone in his corner, someone who'd fight tooth and nail for him, who loved him and would put him first. Suddenly, Mercedes knew that her brother was going to be all right. She nodded briskly, determined not to dwell on it. 'So, what happens now?' she asked crisply.

Oriana sighed. 'If only we could figure out why Margaret killed Rollo. It was the one thing that always nagged at me in prison. Sir Freddy giving me the money smacked of a man trying to ease his conscience, so I always thought that he'd somehow been forced into killing Rollo. I didn't know then that it was Margaret who'd done it. But the question is still the same. Why did *she* kill him?'

'It had to be money,' Mercedes said bitterly. 'Believe me, if Margaret's involved, it has something to do with money.'

Oriana sighed. 'OK, but Rollo didn't have any. Your family was being crippled by inheritance tax, even before Rollo was killed. And the only time Rollo talked about money was as a joke. Lowell told me.' And she told Mercedes about how he'd said the painting in her bedroom was worth a fortune.

Mercedes shook her head. 'Lowell was right. Well, you saw it when I bought it. It's a nice enough amateur daub, but hardly a Rembrandt in disguise.'

'Can I see it?' Oriana asked, more for something to do than anything else. All this talk was getting them nowhere, and she'd been going over and over it so often in her head that she was sick and tired of it.

Mercedes, as if sensing her need for action, smiled. 'Why not. I still have it upstairs. Well, I like it,' she said, laughing.

As the two women climbed the narrow stairs up to Mercedes' room, Connor left the Thames Valley Police Station in Kidlington, confident of some swift action, and headed towards the small village where the Wrights lived. He didn't know it, but he'd missed passing Margaret's car, going in the other direction, by just three minutes.

'There it is,' Mercedes said, theatrically indicating the painting. It was just as Oriana remembered – right down to the illegible signature. A view of Nether Dene, circa 1894. Some of the older cottages were still standing. The cows in the water meadows in the distance still looked rather block-ish. But Oriana rather liked the way the artist had captured the weeping willows on the river. She could see why her friend would be so fond of it. But, with the best will in the world, it was hardly worth a fortune.

'Not even the most avid collector of English bucolic scenes would pay more than a hundred for it,' Oriana said hopelessly.

'Yes, it was like Rollo to say something so daft. He had a weird sense of humour,' Mercedes agreed, her face softening with fond remembrance of her long-gone brother. Then her eyes sharpened. 'Mind you, he usually had some reason for one of his jokes. I mean,' she added, as Oriana looked at her confused, 'he never just said things out of the blue.'

Oriana nodded. 'No. He didn't, did he?' she said thoughtfully. 'I remember once, he said Frances was looking rather blue. And he meant her hands, after she'd spilled that toilet cleaner on them. Do you remember?'

Mercedes laughed. Then looked serious. 'I hope you're going to do something about that Greer woman, Oriana,' she said coldly.

Oriana nodded, her lips twisting. 'Oh yes. Don't worry about that!' Even now, if Connor was right, the police would be checking out Frances Greer very thoroughly.

Perjury was a jailable offence, after all.

But Oriana was in no mood to crow over the immi-nent downfall of her enemies. Instead she was looking at the picture thoughtfully. 'That frame can't be real gold, can it?' she said, extremely doubtfully, and Mercedes laughed, hoisting it off the wall and regarding the painting fondly.

'No it can't!' she laughed. 'It would weigh a ton! But I can see where your thoughts are going – perhaps Rollo meant the painting itself wasn't worth a fortune, but something else about it was.'

'But not the frame!' they both said at once, and then giggled. And suddenly, it was like the old days, before everything had gone so wrong. Two girls, the best of friends, virtual mind-readers, warm and comfortable in each other's company. As their eyes met, they both knew those days had started again. After a break of thirteen years.

'So if it's not the frame,' Mercedes said at last, her heart happily full, turning the painting over to inspect the back, 'perhaps he hid something in it?'

Oriana looked at the back of the painting doubtfully. It was dirty, with a cobweb testifying mutely to Mercedes' rather slipshod attitude to housework, and had a lot of peeling backing paper, turning yellow. Cheap-looking tacks held it all together.

Oriana looked at her friend questioningly. 'Got a blunt knife?'

* * *

Margaret Wright was feeling distinctly up. Too up. She knew her world was falling down around her, and knew, too, that it would only be a matter of time before that damned Oriana Foster put things together. And besides all that, for all she knew, Mercedes was even now telling the cops about how she'd seen her, Margaret, push her into the pool.

Margaret had thought she'd been clever about it, though. She'd been crouched down behind the door, with a deck chair made of tubular steel casing in front of her, and had used that to knock the back of Mercedes' legs and topple her into the water. No feel of arms or fingers. No way for Mercedes to guess at her attacker's identity.

She knew Mercedes couldn't swim, of course, and she'd been careful to keep crouched down behind the chair to keep out of sight as much as possible, but it was still feasible that Mercedes saw her before she went in.

The fact that she didn't drown was proof that Margaret's luck was turning, wasn't it? And she'd always felt, superstitiously, sure of her luck. The fact that it was now changing made her feel savagely desperate. And yet, as the sports car ate up the miles at a reckless pace as she headed towards Nether Dene, she found she was singing the latest pop tune along with the radio, and feeling like she did in the old days, when she was off to Monte Carlo to lose a fortune, or heading to Italy to marry a rich count.

She felt alive.

Probably because she knew she was on the edge. *Really* on the edge. And when a gal was on the edge, she had nothing to lose, right?

She glanced in her rear-view mirror, saw the crossbow and smiled. Well, it might only be a matter of time before the cops came knocking on her door for something or other, but before she went, she was sure as hell going to take that bitch Oriana Foster with her.

No way was she going to let her have Lowell.

She slammed her hand onto the steering wheel and literally screamed with rage.

* * *

'Good grief,' Mercedes said, staring open-mouthed at the piece of paper lying behind the backing paper. 'I never really believed anything would actually be there,' she breathed.

And Oriana knew exactly what she meant. It had been one thing to take the back off the painting, in the spirit of adventure, but it was another thing entirely to have a fantastic hunch pay off. But there it was. A small, square, ancient-looking piece of folded paper.

Mercedes slowly reached her hand out, then drew it back. She looked at Oriana. 'You should do it.'

But Oriana shook her head. 'No. He was your brother.'

Mercedes nodded, carefully swung the dismantled painting onto her bed, and lifted out the piece of paper. If she'd cared to look outside her window at that point, she'd have seen the bright red sports car pull up outside her gate, but her attention was too fixed on the paper in her hand.

'It feels ever so thin,' she said worriedly. 'Really flimsy.'

Oriana watched over her friend's shoulder. The writing was spidery, and almost impossible to read. But at least there wasn't much of it.

'Those letters there – they have to be IOUs don't they?' Mercedes asked doubtfully, and Oriana nodded. It certainly looked like it to her. And something about those initials triggered off a memory. What was it? Something important, she was sure.

She was concentrating so hard, she didn't hear the kitchen door open downstairs.

* * *

In the Dower House Hotel, Lowell finally got away from a couple from Minnesota who wanted his opinion on everything from which of the Oxford colleges was a must see (Christ Church) to which restaurant in Woodstock served the best game. Finally, he was able to wave the loquacious Americans off, and quickly slipped out around the side before any other guests could waylay him.

He had to see Oriana. Since his talk with Connor that morning, which had straightened out so much, he had to see her, to tell her that he loved her.

It wasn't until he was at his sister's gate that he saw the car. Margaret's car.

* * *

'Wait a minute – that's Ebeneezer, isn't it?' Mercedes said, squinting, holding the piece of paper at an angle. 'And the next letter's a capital U—'

'Usted!' Oriana suddenly cried, and so loudly that Margaret, who'd already searched downstairs and found it empty, and was now creeping halfway up the stairs, froze.

So she *was* here.

When she'd stalked into the Manor, openly carrying the crossbow which was now tucked lovingly in her arms, and found the place empty, she'd wondered if the trouble-some blonde interloper was with Lowell at the hotel. If so, she knew she'd have no option but to wait in ambush. But something had told her that Oriana and Mercedes might be together. And so they were. Her old luck hadn't deserted her after all.

Excellent. She grinned widely, maniacally. Two birds with one stone. Or rather, two birds with two crossbow bolts! She continued to edge silently up the stairs.

* * *

Lowell pushed open the gate and walked up the path, a frown on his face. After breaking it off with Margaret yesterday, he'd thought she would keep a low profile. If only for her pride's sake. So what was she doing calling on Mercedes?

He pushed open the kitchen door and looked inside. Empty.

* * *

Upstairs, Mercedes jumped and glanced at her friend. 'What? What's so special about a man called Usted?' Mercedes asked, and on the landing, just outside, Margaret bit back a snarl. So they were on to that already, were they? It was a good job she hadn't wasted any time. She drew back the crossbow and slid a bolt inside. Taking another from the pack, she put it into her deep pocket, ready for a quick reload. She thought she

173

heard a noise downstairs, but it was impossible to tell, with Mercedes and her little friend chattering away like magpies.

'That was what Rollo went to see your great-aunt Agatha about,' Oriana laughed. 'Didn't I tell you?'

Mercedes shook her head.

'Well, Rollo wanted to know about a poker game your great-grandfather got into, oh, several decades ago now. In it he won some land from one Ebeneezer Usted. I remember the name because I searched the county records for it, but there wasn't much there.'

On the landing, Margaret took a deep breath. Steady. Calm. At this distance she couldn't miss.

Downstairs, Lowell heard the sound of female voices, and guessing whose, a grin split his face. He walked out into the hall, and put his foot on the first step.

'Apparently, your ancestor won some land off this Usted person. But when I checked the records, I couldn't find any documentation on any land changing hands between them. I *did* find out that Ebeneezer Usted died that same winter, and that your ancestor died the following spring, so perhaps they didn't get around to officially finalizing it. The only proof was in the IOU, and Rollo must have tracked it down,' Oriana said.

Mercedes nodded. 'And then hid it in the painting. But why?'

'Oh I can tell you that,' Margaret said, stepping into the doorway.

Oriana turned, and froze. Her eyes went straight to the crossbow.

'Margaret, what the hell do you . . .' Mercedes said, taking a step forward, but Oriana quickly pulled her back and stood a little in front of her. Mercedes, only then seeing the crossbow levelled at her, gulped. 'It was you who pushed me in the pool,' she said sharply. So sharply that Lowell, at the foot of the stairs, heard her.

Silently, instinctively knowing that it was crucial, he climbed the stairs as warily as a cat.

'Of course I pushed you in the pool,' Margaret said, mockingly, her voice wild.

Lowell briefly closed his eyes as he recognized the voice, brazenly admitting to the attempt on his sister's life. But he didn't stop to ask himself why. Instinct, again, told him that he didn't have much time. Carefully, he continued climbing.

'After what you said about looking for Rollo's diary, I had to stop you meddling, didn't I?' Margaret said, her voice sounding hideously reasonable. It was at that point that Oriana realized the woman was quite mad. 'What if you'd found them?' Margaret continued, her eyes wide in mock hypothesis. 'They might have told you all about *that* then,' she concluded, and nodded towards the slip of paper, still clutched in Mercedes' hand. 'By the way,' she sneered contemptuously, 'thank you for finding it for me. You wouldn't believe how long I've been trying to get my hands on it. It's been a thorn in my flesh for years. I've always been scared it would turn up some time, in Rollo's things. After his funeral I was on tenterhooks for months. It was intolerable. Here, give it to me,' she said imperiously, holding out her hand.

'Don't give it to her,' Oriana said sharply, but Mercedes was already holding it protectively behind her back.

Margaret, seeing the way the crossbow wavered when held only in one hand, hastily took her hand back to steady her weapon. She shrugged. 'No matter. I'll just collect it later, and burn it.'

Oriana's blood turned cold as she said the word 'later'. Because she knew what it meant. Margaret intended to kill them both. And she had no idea what to do about it. Oh, why hadn't she asked Connor to come with her? Now, just when they needed him the most?

She had no idea what to do except play for time, and hope Connor came back. Margaret was too far away for Oriana to attempt to rush her, and besides, she was deadly accurate with any bow and arrow, *that* she already knew. At this distance, it would be suicide.

'But what's so important about an old IOU, Margaret?' she asked, not knowing that Lowell, too, was desperate to hear the answer, that he was, even now, less than a few yards away, creeping up on Margaret, knowing every question that had plagued him since Oriana's wonderful return was going to be answered.

'The land, of course,' Margaret sneered. 'What else? Rollo thought he was being so clever. But he didn't count on me.' She crowed so exultantly that Mercedes' head lifted defiantly.

She, like Oriana, had understood that Margaret had gone totally berserk, and really was planning to kill them both in cold blood. And, also like Oriana, she was terrified.

She'd managed to ease herself around so that she was standing beside her friend, rather than just a little behind her. She wanted to thank Oriana for trying to protect her, but she couldn't let her risk her own life at the cost of hers.

But now the mention of Rollo replaced some of the fear with anger. 'What do you mean? What did Rollo do?' she asked, her defiance making Margaret laugh.

'Well, well, well, the little princess has some spunk after all. Well, let me tell you, your big brother was no knight on a white charger. He was nothing more than a blackmailing, greedy little cretin. I soon fixed him!'

Lowell was at the door now. He had no idea what the situation was inside, but again instinct stopped him from just charging in. He chanced a quick peek around the door. Luckily for both Oriana and Mercedes, who couldn't help but gape with relief when they saw his face, Margaret was too enraged and indignant to notice their sudden shift in eye movement, and a distinct heightening of the tension.

'Dad was building his first supermarket, you see,' Margaret said, bringing both girls' attention back to her. 'Out near Banbury. Close enough to town to be convenient, but still out in the sticks enough to get all the tax benefits. He'd bought the land from Gabriel Usted, the local farmer, in good faith. It was already half-built when who should come a-calling but Rollo Seton, with a photocopy of that lit-tle document there,' Margaret sneered, 'proving that the land didn't really belong to Usted at all, but to the Seton family.'

Oriana slowly let out a breath. Her mind was racing. Lowell was there, but unarmed. She needed to keep Margaret distracted, and be ready to move when he did.

'But surely it wasn't legal?' Mercedes said. 'I mean, after all this time. And a hand-written IOU, from a poker game years ago – why didn't you just hire a lawyer to fight it?' Mercedes demanded. 'Why did you have to *kill* him?'

Margaret laughed. Actually laughed. And as she did so, Lowell stepped from the landing and through the doorway. Margaret's back, directly in front of him, was as tensely held as the crossbow string she was fingering teasingly.

'Oh, what did it matter whether or not it was *legal?*' Margaret hissed. 'If we'd gone through the courts, Dad would have lost everything anyway, even if they did finally come down on his side. You can't halt the building of a huge supermarket just like that! There were building contracts in place, penalties to be considered. And your Rollo knew that. He'd got Dad over a barrel, and he knew it. That's why he came to the house and demanded two million. *Two million*! As if Dad had that kind of money to hand back then.'

Lowell took another step towards her, craning his head a little to the right to get a better look at the weapon she was carrying. It looked all set and primed and ready to go. And it was pointing right at Oriana.

Both women, realizing that their lives depended on not giving the game away, kept their eyes firmly fixed on Margaret, sheer force of will preventing them from looking over her shoulder at Lowell. Fortunately, Margaret was too intent on venting her spleen to notice what was going on.

'But Dad wasn't there that night. I was,' she mused. 'And I saw the danger at once. I knew Dad would be appalled to think that he'd bought land which really belonged to someone else, and being the damned straight-laced softie he is, might even have agreed to give you Setons a cut of the profits to stop any lawsuits. Well, I couldn't have that, could I? That was my inheritance he'd be cutting into. So I thought fast, and promised Rollo that I'd talk to Dad, and assured him he'd get his money. But instead, I waited until he'd gone, then followed him home. It was easy. No one was around. I meant to seduce him, and then steal the IOU, but he must have already hidden it before I got there.' Margaret's face contorted in remembered rage. 'And then he made love to me, and afterwards laughed in my face. Said he was *still* going to ask for the two million. The worm! So I pushed him.' Margaret tossed her head arrogantly, not a trace of remorse on her expertly made-up face. 'We were at the top of the stairs by then. I'd got dressed, and he was watching me like a cat that had got the cream. But he didn't laugh after he'd gone down the stairs,' she finished, her voice rich in satisfaction.

Mercedes felt sick.

Lowell, who was debating the best way to get hold of the crossbow before she could fire it, went white and tight-lipped as Margaret cold-bloodedly laughed about the murder of his brother, but he didn't let his anger distract him. There was no way he could just grab the weapon – she might fire it instinctively, and at this range it was bound to hit Oriana.

No, there was only one thing he could do.

'I didn't know that your damned housekeeper was there, did I?' Margaret carried on, looking at Mercedes venomously, as if it were her fault. 'When I got to the bottom of the stairs, I saw her in the kitchen doorway. Of course, I had to shut her up. Pay her off. It was then that I realized I needed a scape-goat. The coroner was bound to find bruises on him from where I'd pushed him. It was then that I remembered he was going out with you,' Margaret said, sneering at Oriana. 'Little Miss Nobody. Who'd care about you? So I paid the housekeeper to tell a few lies in court. The rest, as they say, is history. And now . . .' She moved the crossbow a fraction of an inch, and Oriana felt death appear at her shoulder.

Lowell moved. His hands came around Margaret's waist, moving up in a hard, chopping motion. Margaret cried out in pain as the blows hit her, forcing the crossbow up. As it did, there was a deadly *whish* followed by a *thunk* as the bolt shot harmlessly into the ceiling above them.

Margaret began to scream obscenities.

Oriana and Mercedes clung to one another as Lowell, grim-faced, grabbed the bow from her grip and tossed it harmlessly onto the bed, then grabbed Margaret's wrists and spun her around to face him, murder in his eyes.

'Lowell, don't!' Oriana cried sharply. 'She's not worth it.'

'She killed Rollo and framed you,' Lowell panted, his face white with the fear he only now allowed himself to feel. 'And she was going to kill you. Both of you.'

Margaret laughed. It was a loud, hideous laugh.

'But she didn't. You saved us,' Oriana said, letting go of Mercedes to come quickly to his side. 'Lowell, if you hurt her now, you'll go to prison too. And we've been apart for long enough. Haven't we?' She put her hand on his shoulder. 'Haven't we?' she repeated softly.

Lowell blinked and shook his head. He looked at Margaret, who was staring back at him scornfully, a sneer on her lips, but with something desperate in her eyes.

Then he looked at Oriana. Her blue eyes begging him.

'You're right,' he said, nodding.

And Oriana slowly let out her breath and leaned her face to rest against the back of his shoulder.

'I'll go call the police,' Mercedes said shakily, and left the room on legs which felt like rubber.

FOURTEEN

Oriana stepped back from the Christmas tree, a gold foil snowflake in one hand, and, cocking her head to one side, she looked at the big fir thoughtfully.

The living room had been one of the first rooms in the old Manor House to be redecorated, after the plumbers and electricians, glaziers and carpet layers had finished. She rather liked the ivory walls, turquoise and emerald green accents, and big black leather armchairs and sofa. Now, with the Christmas tree in place beside the glowing log fire, the room was even further transformed.

She sighed at the thought of the decorators returning in the New Year, but for now, she and Lowell had the place to themselves.

She had a huge turkey waiting in the fridge for tomorrow, for Mercedes and Connor had been invited, along with some other mutual friends, for Christmas dinner.

It was hard to believe that so many things could change in just six months.

But Margaret Wright was in prison for the murder of Rollo Seton, and the attempted murders of Oriana and Mercedes. She might have been sharing a cell with Frances

Greer, if the one-time housekeeper hadn't been sent to another jail down south. Oriana's full pardon hadn't got free of all the red tape yet, but everyone knew it was just a matter of time. Connor and Mercedes were engaged and due to be married in April. Mercedes kept threatening to have the cottage expanded, especially the bathroom, but Connor was trying to talk her round. He rather liked being squashed into the shower with her, or so he kept saying.

Fred Wright had died before his daughter could come to trial, and Margaret was still fighting an action to have his last will overturned, but nobody believed she'd win.

Mercedes and Lowell had talked it over when they learned they were the beneficiaries of Fred's will, along with Oriana.

Lowell was determined to give any money which came his way to charity, not wanting to have anything to do with the Wrights ever again. It was understandable, and Oriana felt proud of him for it. Besides, with his head for business, she knew that Lowell was perfectly capable of earning his own fortune – in fact, he was already well on the way.

But for her it was different. She felt as if she'd earned her money, or rather, had a moral right to it, and so she was keeping the Manor, and using the rest of her fortune to refurbish it and bring it back to its former glory.

Lowell had no objection. He, too, believed she deserved the best, and if it meant moving back into his beloved family home, and one day raising their kids there, as he and Mercedes had been raised there, who was he to object?

Mercedes hadn't decided yet what to do if and when her inheritance came her way. But she was threatening to drag Connor away with her on a year-long world cruise for a start, in order to think it over in comfort. He was still pretending to dislike the idea. Watching them argue was always good fun, and Oriana was looking forward to having them over tomorrow.

She turned as she heard the door open, and Lowell walked in.

He looked at the tree and grinned. 'Is there a fir underneath all that?' he asked, and Oriana looked back and laughed.

'Perhaps I overdid the tinsel a bit.'

'Just a bit.'

He came to stand behind her, his arms going around her waist, his dark head next to her fair one, and contemplated the tree. 'I hope you tried the fairy lights to see if they worked before you draped them over the branches,' he said warningly, and Oriana sighed.

'I *knew* there was something I forgot!'

She watched as Lowell bent down to put in the plug. He looked so good, dressed in a black cable-knit sweater and an old pair of jeans.

They never talked about the past now, after that day when Margaret had tried to kill them. It was as if those few fraught minutes had laid to rest every ghost which might haunt them in the future. And Oriana was glad. Her life was too full, too busy, too active, to think about what was gone. The past was over and done with, as far as they were concerned.

Lowell was teaching her to drive, with marvellous patience and skill, and she was taking a course in bookkeeping. She hoped, one day, to be able to help Lowell in his business. Perhaps go halves with him to buy a second hotel. Who knows, perhaps they'd start a chain together?

'*Voila!*' Lowell said, as the tree lit up with tiny orbs of pink, blue, green, gold, white and purple.

Night was just beginning to fall outside as once more he put his arms around her, the lights from the Christmas tree spreading colour across their faces.

Lowell slowly turned his head to hers, tipping her chin back and kissing her.

'I love you,' he said.

Oriana nodded. 'Yes,' she said softly. She knew. She didn't need to tell him she loved him too. They both knew it.

And from now on, no matter what happened, it would never be doubted.

They had lived through the worst that life could throw at them. The danger was gone, and all the lies were forgotten. Now, the future beckoned.

Their future. Together.

THE END

Thank you for reading this book. If you enjoyed it please leave feedback on Amazon or Goodreads, and if there is anything we missed or you have a question about, then please get in touch. The author and publishing team appreciate your feedback and time reading this book.

We're very grateful to eagle-eyed readers who take the time to contact us. Please send any errors you find to corrections@joffebooks.com